MW00809823

Have Ears

A Black Spy in The Confederate White House

Hope Irvin Marston

White Bird Publications
P.O. Box 90145
Austin, Texas 78709
http://www.whitebirdpublications.com

Copyright©2018—Hope Irvin Marston
Cover design: E. Kusch

ISBN: 978-1-63363-347-6
LCCN: 2018959469

PRINTED IN THE UNITED STATES OF AMERICA

DEDICATION

TO JERRY

Acknowledgments

My thanks to Rosemarie Hare, Jefferson Community College Library, Watertown, NY, for the many reference books she secured for me through ILL.

This book could never have been completed had it not been for the encouragement I received from my Critique Group: Aline Newman, Judyann Grant, and Jule Lattimer, through many years of rewrites.

It would not have found a publisher had it not been whipped into shape in its early stages by the expertise of Ranelda Hunsaker and in its final version by Mary Blount Christian.

The Walls Have Ears

A Black Spy in The Confederate White House

White Bird Publications

Chapter One

Richmond, VA 1845

Late one summer morning, Mary Jane Richards skipped into the parlor and peered through the lacey white curtains covering the broad window of the three-story mansion where she lived with Miss Bet Van Lew. The majestic old house sat diagonally across from the imposing St. John's Episcopal Church, occupying a whole block atop Church Hill overlooking the city of Richmond.

Mary Jane strained to catch a glimpse of the Van

Lews' four snowy-white horses. Soon they would be drawing Miss Bet home in her shiny black carriage with its silky lining and soft velvety seats.

Mary Jane couldn't remember her momma, or the days before Miss Bet began taking care of her. One afternoon when she was five, she said to one of the older slaves, "Wilson, what happened to my momma?"

Wilson gathered her soft hands into his and looked into her dark eyes. He paused, blinked, and swallowed before answering. "Mary Jane, yer momma took sick and died when ya was two years old. From that day on Miss Bet took care of ya jist as if ya was her little girl." Blinking again, he added, "When you wuz three, Miss Bet gave all us slaves our freedom papers. That meant we could leave Church Hill." A broad smile lit up his face. "Most of us wanted ta stay, so she kept us on and began ta pay us servants' wages."

Mary Jane thought again about what Wilson told her as she stared out the window. What she remembered about the day Miss Bet freed them was the corncob doll Wilson made for her. She still carried it in her pocket most everywhere she went. Sometimes, she hid it in her bedroom in a secret place.

Today Miss Bet was away for a late morning visit with the governor's wife. "You and I will have a tea party when I return," she promised. She gave her a motherly hug before stepping up into her carriage.

Mary Jane was thinking about the tea party when off in the distance she spied the team of horses making its way home. She bolted out the huge oak door, streaked down the curved steps, and charged out through the iron gate. She waited at her post, enchanted by the graceful horses clip-clopping their way up the cobblestones to Church Hill. When they reached the top, Wilson halted them in front of the majestic brick and stucco mansion and set the brake.

The handsome animals lowered their heads one by one as Mary Jane called them by name. "I love you," she whispered as she gave each horse a huge hug. Meanwhile, Wilson stepped down from his box seat in front of the barouche. He extended his gloved hand and helped Miss Bet alight. Before driving the horses to the carriage house, he paused and gave Mary Jane's cornrow braids a gentle tug.

Miss Bet opened her arms and engulfed the child in a warm embrace. Then, taking her hand, they climbed the long staircase together. "First, we shall have our tea," she said. "After that, we must get to work."

Mary Jane beamed. Though she was only seven, one of her favorite things was learning to take her tea with Miss Bet, like a grand Richmond lady.

The two of them seated themselves comfortably at

a Queen Anne side table between the upholstered wing chairs in the drawing room. Hannah, the kitchen maid, entered shortly to serve them. Wearing her blue-gray dress with the spotless white pinner apron, she carried a Sterling silver tray laden with tea and fresh pastries. Mary Jane's mouth watered when she saw the dainty tea cakes, gingerbread nuts, and especially the lemon tarts.

After pouring Miss Bet's tea, Hannah filled Mary Jane's cup.

"Thank you, ma'am," Mary Jane said. Remembering what Miss Bet had taught her, she picked it up, being careful not to extend her little finger.

When their tea party ended, Miss Bet excused herself and left the drawing room. She returned within a few minutes with a feather duster. "Now it's time for us to get busy," she said, handing it to Mary Jane. "Today, I want you to dust both parlors."

"Yes, Miss Bet," Mary Jane said as Hannah gathered up their teacups and returned to the kitchen. She picked up the duster and headed to the larger parlor.

Bright sunlight streamed in through the high windows onto the crystal chandeliers making them sparkle like giant diamonds. Mary Jane paused to admire them. Then, as she slowly swished the duster across the polished furniture, she amused herself by reciting aloud a Bible story she'd learned when she went to church with

Caroline, the Van Lews' cook.

"Now, baby Moses, he be a fine child. His momma knew that, and so she wanted to hide him from mean old Pharaoh. So she made him a little bitty basket. Then, she covered it with tar and set that bitty basket in thuh river. Before long…"

She was in the middle of her story when she heard Miss Bet running down the long hallway to the parlor. She charged into the room and grabbed Mary Jane by the shoulders with such force she dropped her duster.

"Mary Jane," she shouted. "In Virginia, it's against the law for blacks to learn to read. If anyone finds out you know how, they'll take you away from me and throw me in jail. Tell me, child, WHO taught you to read that story?"

Mary Jane cowered at her words. Tears streamed down her cheeks. Miss Bet had never shouted at her or laid a harsh hand on her. "Nobody taught me, Miss Bet. Please, don't let them take me away." She quivered.

"Then how do you know that story?"

"I heard it first when Cook took me to church," Mary Jane said, speaking through her sobs. She swallowed her tears. "Then, I heard it again last year…that day you took me to be baptized at your church."

Mary Jane' face paled as the memory of the day

5

Miss Bet dared to take her to the mostly white Saint John's Episcopal Church flooded her mind. That morning, Miss Bet picked up some bright red beads from her dresser and braided them into cornrows. She loved Miss Bet's beads, but that was the first time she'd put them into her hair. "Why are you fixing my hair so pretty this morning?" she'd asked.

Miss Bet finished the last braid and reached for Mary Jane's hand. "Today I'm taking you to my church."

Panicked at her words, Mary Jane drew back from her. "Why isn't Cook taking me to church with her?"

Miss Bet knelt down to her eye level. "Mary Jane, after your momma died, I became your momma." She pulled her into a warm hug. "I love you as though you were my very own child. I want you to be with me in my church from now on."

Mary Jane quivered. "But…but…only white people go there. I'm scared."

Miss Bet shook her head. "That's not true, Mary Jane. You'll see other little girls there just like you."

"But the big people won't want me to come to their church." She stared wide-eyed at Miss Bet. What if…?"

Miss Bet wrapped her arms around her tighter. "St. John's has been my family's church since before I was born," she said. "I was baptized there. My sister Anna and my brother John were, also. My father was an important businessman in Richmond, and he gave lots of money to the church. Mary Jane, you are my child, and I have every right to take you with me. No one will harm you." She looked into Mary Jane's eyes and spoke softly. "Now that you are seven-years-old, I've arranged for you to be baptized today."

Mary Jane didn't know what it meant to be baptized, and she was too frightened to ask. She squirmed and pleaded to be allowed to go to church with the other freed slaves in the Van Lew household.

Miss Bet shook her head. "You'll be safe sitting with me." She straightened one of Mary Jane's cornrow braids a bit and then smoothed her own hair. After tying her prettiest bonnet under her chin, she picked up her parasol. Reaching for Mary Jane's hand, she said, "Come, child, it's time we made our way to St. John's."

Though a year had passed since that frightful day, Mary Jane remembered every detail as if it had happened last week. She had held tight to Miss Bet's hand as they left their Church Hill mansion and walked across the street to St. John's Episcopal Church.

She felt dwarfed as they entered the churchyard which was surrounded by a wooden fence taller than she was. As they stepped inside the church house, she drew back at the sight of such a huge place. Instead of crude benches, there were boxed-in little rooms with doors on them where people sat to worship. In one corner down front, there was a big organ with pipes towering above it.

Miss Bet opened one of the little doors and took her inside. As they sat down in the pew the Van Lew family had rented for many years, the women nearby scowled. Once seated, Miss Bet pointed down front to a white marble stand with a large bowl on top of it. "That's the baptismal font," she whispered. Then she explained to Mary Jane how she would be baptized that morning.

Just as Mary Jane feared, some of the women didn't want her there. They whispered loud enough for most everyone in the large congregation to hear: *"What is she doing in OUR church? Miss Bet has no business bringing one of her slaves here. I don't want her near my children."* One angry woman looked down her long nose, pointed a crooked finger at her, and gritted her teeth.

When the rector announced that Mary Jane was to be baptized that morning, the nasty remarks grew louder. Mary Jane held her breath and trembled like a quivering aspen tree.

Miss Bet had pulled her close, using both hands to calm her fears. "You're my daughter now, Mary Jane," she whispered. "From now on, I want you to be with me in church just like other little girls are with their mommas."

To avoid attracting attention, Mary Jane sat still as a rock staring at the baptismal font as the congregation sang unfamiliar hymns. When the rector began telling a story from the Bible, she slid toward the edge of her seat, not missing a word. Later at home, she remembered the songs and recited the story inside her head.

At the appropriate time in the service, Miss Bet took her hand and led her to the front of the church. Mary Jane held her breath as the rector prayed for her and then sprinkled a few droplets of water on her head.

Nobody harmed her that first morning, but Mary Jane was too afraid to relax. Though Miss Bet held tightly to her hand as they walked home at the close of the services, her heart pounded with each step. Once inside, Miss Bet drew her close to her heart until eventually, she calmed down.

That afternoon, Wilson found a piece of old wood and carved a top for her. He brought it to her and taught her how to make it spin. It became her favorite toy, and she kept it in her apron pocket along with her corncob doll. Whenever she was afraid or upset, she pulled it out and played with it.

Despite the comments and behavior of many of the women at St. John's, Miss Bet insisted that Mary Jane accompany her to church every Sunday thereafter. Now she reached into her pocket and fingered her doll with her right hand. She smiled, remembering that Wilson had made it especially for her. She felt loved and that calmed her enough, so she could tell Miss Bet how she learned the story of Baby Moses.

She snuffled trying to hold her tears inside. "I liked that story about baby Moses," she said. "So, I've been telling it to myself." She looked at Miss Bet. "Miss Bet, I cain't read. But I've a good memory; that's all."

"Do you remember any other stories?"

"Yes, Miss Bet," she stammered.

"Tell me another one."

Mary Jane stared at her shoes and recited the story of David and Goliath. When she finished, she looked up into Miss Bet's face. It had softened a little, and she let go of her shoulders. Still, she looked puzzled.

"Do you remember any stories besides the ones you've heard in church?"

Mary Jane shuddered and avoided looking at her.

Miss Bet spoke again, in the kind, gentle voice that she was used to hearing. "Mary Jane, what else do you remember?"

"I remember *everything* I hear. *And see*. Cook and Hannah taught me to be quiet when I am with white people, so I just tell the stories inside my head. Today I forgot and talked out loud." She grasped Miss Bet's hands. "Please, don't let anyone take me away from you."

Miss Bet drew her near, looked around, and then nodded toward the settee. "Let's sit down."

Once they were seated, she pulled her close. "Mary Jane, you are the smartest little girl I've ever known." She held her tight until the trembling ceased. "I'm sorry I frightened you." She paused, as though choosing her words carefully. "Because you are a black child, it *is* against the law for anyone to teach you to read."

She drew in several deep breaths. "But that is an unfair law. I love you, child," she said, wrapping her arms around her. "You deserve to be able to learn." She set her jaw and added, "No matter what the law says, I *will* teach you to read. But that must be our secret." She lowered her voice. "You must *never* let anyone know you have learned. If you do, I will be taken to jail."

Tears clouded Mary Jane's eyes, and she shook her head. "No, Miss Bet. I don't want to learn." She gulped. "It will get you into trouble…and they'll take you away."

"That will never happen, my precious child. We will keep it a secret between us." Miss Bet cradled her close once more. "Mary Jane, I have loved you and cared for you for five years. I don't ever want to be separated from you." She paused. "Your skin may be darker than mine, but you are *my* child. I will always take care of you." She reached down, gently wiped her tears, and kissed her forehead.

Once Mary Jane calmed down, Miss Bet said, "Sometimes God gives us special gifts just because we are His children, and He loves us. And so that we can help others." She looked directly into Mary Jane's face. "Being able to remember what you see and hear is God's special gift to you. You must keep that gift a secret between us, so I don't get into trouble."

"But why would God give me a gift that could get you into trouble, Miss Bet?"

Miss Bet kissed her forehead. "Someday, He will show you how to use it."

Still holding her close, she added in a hushed voice. "Our special relationship with each other would get me into trouble only if anyone in Richmond found out about it." She breathed deeply. "We must keep it a secret within our household forever, as well as your ability to remember what you see and hear." She looked intently into Mary Jane's face and then kissed her cheek. "Do you understand what I am saying?"

"Yes, Miss Bet," she whispered.

One morning about a month later as Mary Jane was finishing her morning kitchen chores, Miss Bet called her into the parlor. Kneeling on the hearth, she beckoned her to come close. "My precious child, you have been given a rare gift. I *will not* let it go to waste." She looked at her and said, "Watch me." Using her forefinger, she wrote in the ashes, 'MARY JANE.'

Mary Jane stared into the ashes as Miss Bet pointed to each of the letters, naming them one by one. "M A R Y J A N E." Then she spoke the words aloud.

Mary Jane watched her wide-eyed. "That's my name," she whispered.

A few days later, Miss Bet gave her the first daily reading lesson using a slate and chalk. Mary Jane wanted to learn to read, and she caught on fast. But she never forgot Miss Bet's grave warning. *My life with Miss Bet depends on no one ever finding out I can read. But what if someone, somehow, discovers my secret? What then?*

Chapter Two

About a month later, Miss Bet called Mary Jane into the kitchen. "You've done a good job in dusting the parlors this morning," she said. "Would you like to go to the market with me?"

"Oh, yes," Mary Jane said. She enjoyed going places with Miss Bet. Most mornings Miss Bet went out to do her errands alone, so this would be a treat. Mary Jane took her hand, and they left the mansion together.

Instead of heading directly to the market, they took the route through Shockhoe Bottom and Lumpkin's Alley. Mary Jane had never been in this section of

Richmond because it was the place where slave owners conducted their business. Miss Bet held her close as she scanned the posted notices about runaway slaves. They paused briefly where a small red sign hung on a post outside an open door.

Inside, chains clanked as a terrified young man was led to the auction block. The auctioneer began pointing out the selling points of his "human goods" as he called out for larger bids. When he could not raise a higher one, he struck the block with a loud bang. Mary Jane jumped when he yelled, "SOLD." Never had she seen anyone look so terrified as that poor captive. She swallowed and grabbed Miss Bet's hand with both of hers, as Miss Bet led her away from the frightening place. She couldn't stop shaking until they reached the market, did their shopping, and returned home to their Church Hill mansion.

A year had passed since Mary Jane began learning to read. One afternoon after she had finished her dusting chores, Miss Bet called to her from the kitchen. "I need your help to carry some things up to the attic," she said. She held out a small basket for her while she picked up a second one.

Mary Jane wrinkled her nose at the aroma drifting out from the heated crock inside her basket. "That smells like what we ate for lunch a little while ago," she said. "Why are we carrying warm food up to the attic?"

Miss Bet did not answer her question.

Mary Jane had never before climbed to the third floor of the mansion. When they got to the attic, the stairs opened into a very long hall. Miss Bet set her basket down near a dresser that stood along the wall. She motioned for Mary Jane to do the same with the one she was carrying. "Help me pull this dresser away from the wall," she said.

Once they moved the heavy chest, Mary Jane saw what looked like a small, whitewashed, square door behind where the chest stood. The door fit flush against the wall, but it had no knob and no hinges.

Miss Bet stooped down and knocked softly on the "door." Very slowly it opened from the inside. A black man peered out, a look of expectation covering his face.

"We've brought you some warm food, Sam," Miss Bet said, handing him her basket.

As Mary Jane passed her basket over to the stranger, shafts of sunlight streamed into the secret room from small windows high above the street. Curious, she strained to see inside, but the stranger filled the doorway, and she saw nothing more.

"I'm working out the safest route to get you to Philadelphia," Miss Bet said to the man. "I expect to hear from one of my couriers this evening. As soon as I know the plan, I'll return to tell you."

"Thank yuh, Miz Bet," the runaway replied, grinning. He disappeared inside and closed the door. As Mary Jane helped Miss Bet push the dresser back in place, the latch inside the room clicked.

Questions tumbled about in Mary Jane's mind as she followed Miss Bet down the stairs to the kitchen on the first floor. Before she could ask them, Miss Bet pulled her close and whispered, "Now you and I have a third secret, Mary Jane."

Mid-morning, about a week later, Miss Bet sent Mary Jane to the basement to get some dried fruit. In her eagerness to please, she tripped as she ran down the steps. Wilson had just come into the kitchen when she fell. Hearing her cries, he hastened to see what happened. At first glance, he could tell that she'd hurt her leg. He spoke softly to her as he picked her up and carried her up the stairs to Miss Bet.

While Cook and Hannah helped take care of Mary Jane's broken leg, Wilson slipped away to find something to comfort her. Looking around the yard, he found two walnut shells which he fashioned into a moon winder. By the time he returned to the kitchen, Mary

Jane had calmed down a bit. Wilson gave her the moon winder and showed her how to make it spin. Once she learned to do that, her new little toy helped her forget her pain and Wilson went back to his work.

Spring, 1849

Born a slave in the Van Lew mansion, Mary Jane had learned from the other slaves the importance of pretending to be ignorant whenever white people were present. Her life with Miss Bet depended on no one, not even those in the Van Lew household, finding out that she could read and write. So, she didn't speak unless someone asked her a question. And even then, she used as few words as possible.

One afternoon as she and Miss Bet were again having tea in the drawing room, Miss Bet said, "Mary Jane, now that you've learned to read and write, I want you to get an education." She returned her teacup to the silver tray and looked directly at her. "You are not an ordinary child, and you deserve to go to school. Since the law prohibits you from being taught here in Richmond, I've made secret plans to send you north to Philadelphia."

Mary Jane's jaw dropped, and she held her teacup

midair, mesmerized by what Miss Bet was saying. "To Philadelphia. That is far away, Miss Bet. I don't want to leave you."

"If you grow up here on Church Hill, you'll learn only what I have time to teach you secretly. My sister Anna has invited you to come live with her and her husband, Dr. Joseph Klapp. She will enroll you in a school in Philadelphia." Though Mary Jane quaked at her words, Miss Bet continued. "Please, hear me out, Mary Jane. Black people are free to live where they want to in Philadelphia. There are schools where you will be welcome to come and learn. You won't have to hide from anyone. And, just in case you should be questioned, I'll make sure you have up-to-date papers, declaring you are a free black."

As the full impact of what Miss Bet was saying hit home, Mary Jane gasped. *How could she ever live without Miss Bet and Wilson, taking care of her*? Her china teacup crashed to the floor, breaking into pieces. She stared saucer-eyed at Miss Bet. Her stomach clenched into a tight ball. It seemed like a cold fist was closing in over her heart, and she grimaced as if in pain. "No, Miss Bet. I'm afraid to leave you." She grabbed Miss Bet's hands and knelt at her feet.

Miss Bet released her hands and laid them gently on Mary Jane's shoulders. "Look at me, Mary Jane," she said. "Other blacks are not so fortunate. It's time for you to nourish your special gift. Don't you want all children, whatever their color, to learn to read? To be free to walk the streets without fear? To be able to speak openly and not have to pretend to be mindless and thick-headed when with white people?"

Mary Jane thought about the horrors of the slave auction she had seen. And also the abuse of blacks that was common in the streets of Richmond. She wished that could be brought to an end. But that didn't calm her dread of leaving her home in Church Hill and the people who loved her and cared for her.

"Please…please…please," she pleaded. "You promised you'd never send me away." She choked on the air rushing into her throat and clung to Miss Bet's knees with trembling hands.

Miss Bet swallowed her threatening tears and pulled Mary Jane into her arms until she stopped sobbing. Then, lifting Mary Jane's chin with a gentle hand, she said, "I love you, Mary Jane. That's why I want you to go where you can learn things that you can't be taught here in Virginia."

Miss Bet drew in a long breath and continued speaking softly. "You'll be safe with Miss Anna and her husband. Your studies will be easy, because you remember everything you see and hear. Once you settle in with them, you'll find many interesting things to read and do in Philadelphia."

She held her close with one arm while tracing circles of comfort on her back until Mary Jane's sobs subsided. "Mary Jane, you are my child, and I love you very much." She kissed her brow and continued in a soft voice. "I'll miss you every day that you are away from us. But it would be wrong to ignore your gifted mind. I'll send you letters with news from home as often as I can. I promise you that when the time is right, I will come for you and bring you home again."

Mary Jane burst into tears and buried her head in Miss Bet's comforting arms. She did not want to leave her to go north and live with people she'd never met. She shuddered as Miss Bet talked about it. "Miss Anna loves children," she said. "She and her husband have five daughters of their own."

That night Mary cried herself to sleep, hoping Miss Bet would change her mind about sending her to Philadelphia.

Chapter Three

Despite her tears and her fearful misgivings, Mary Jane could not change Miss Bet's mind. She lost no time in arranging to send her north. A few days later a young black couple arrived at her Church Hill home. "Mary Jane, these are my friends, Bob and Liza Green."

"Hello, Mary Jane," Liza said.

Hannah served them tea in the drawing room as they sat around the table to discuss the plans for Mary Jane's travel to Philadelphia.

"We can take you safely to Miss Anna's house," Bob said.

Mary Jane stared at him through bleary eyes.

"Just to be safe, we'll travel much of the way at night," he added. "That way we're less likely to be seen."

Just to be safe? More fear gripped Mary Jane's stomach, and her face turned ashen.

Liza laid a comforting hand on her. "Don't be afraid. We'll take good care of you." She looked into her face. "This will be our ninth trip north, taking our people to freedom, and nobody has ever stopped us." She nodded toward her husband and continued. "We don't expect any trouble. If we are stopped and questioned, we'll show our free papers."

Mary Jane's stomach felt like a gigantic ball of tangled fears that she'd never be able to shake loose. *I want to learn. But I've never been away from Miss Bet. I don't know the people in Philadelphia. I don't know when I can come back. I don't want to go.* She turned to Miss Bet with tears streaming down her face. "Please, don't send me away."

Miss Bet drew her close and held her there until her trembling ceased. "Mary Jane, I know this frightens you. I'm sorry I can't take you to Miss Anna's myself. But you deserve to get an education. I'm sending you to her because I love you, child."

"If I have to go, then why can't Wilson take me?"

Miss Bet smiled. "Wilson loves you, too, Mary Jane, and he wants what's best for you. But he doesn't have your gifted mind." She drew in several long breaths. "If I thought I'd never see you again, I wouldn't let you out of my sight."

"We'll be back for you at dusk the day after tomorrow," Liza said, putting an arm around Mary Jane. "I'll keep you company along the way to Philadelphia. Once you get there, Miss Anna and her husband will make you feel right at home."

Two evenings later, Bob and Liza returned by horse and carriage as planned. Miss Bet welcomed them and introduced them to Wilson. When Mary Jane saw them, she ran to her room and threw herself onto her bed. She looked up at the sound of Wilson's voice. He was kneeling beside her.

She raised her head and looked at him through her tears. "I don't want to go to Miss Anna's." She choked. "Miss Bet promised she would never send me away."

Wilson took her small hands into his and sighed softly. "I know ya cain't understand it now, Mary Jane. Miss Bet wants ya ta go ta Philadelphia, so ya can go ta school." He struggled to get his words out. "We'll all miss ya. Someday, ya will come back home ta us." He laid his hand on her shoulder and added, "When ya feel lonely, look at the toys I made for ya. Then ya will feel our love for ya." He blinked, swallowed, and took her hand, leading her back to the others.

The farewells were brief, but tearful, especially for Mary Jane as she said goodbye to Miss Bet, Cook, Hannah, and Wilson. Wilson lifted her up into the carriage and patted her hand. Along with the others, he waved until they were out of sight.

Inside the carriage, Mary Jane sobbed uncontrollably. Though Liza held her close for hours, she cried for many a mile of their journey.

In due time, the exhausted travelers reached Philadelphia. The Klapps welcomed Mary Jane to their home with warm greetings. When Miss Anna reached out and wrapped her in a gentle hug, she burst into tears. Speaking softly, Miss Anna said, "Mary Jane, our little girls have grown up. We miss them. We wished we had another little girl. And now *you* have come to live with us." As she held her close, Mary Jane noticed she had gentle eyes like Miss Bet's. When she sheltered in her in her comforting arms, her touch felt like Miss Bet's.

Taking her hand, she said, "Let me show you the room we've prepared for you." She led her down a short hallway, pausing at the first door on the left. "This is our library," she said, giving her a glance inside. "You may go in there at any time. But first I want to show you your room." She nodded toward the open door on the right.

Mary Jane peered into a cozy room with a small fireplace. Bright sunshine poured through double-windows between the fluffy white curtains, filling the room with warmth. A bright blue quilt covered the single bed which occupied one wall, next to a small closet. Along the opposite wall stood a desk with several drawers and a chair with a flowered cushion on it. A tall oil lamp with a bright blue globe stood on the desk next to a large sign that said, "WELCOME MARY JANE."

As Mary Jane turned to the right, she saw a child's rocking chair. On it sat a large rag doll in a bright red dress with matching bows in her cornrow braids. Miss Anna smiled as Mary Jane grabbed up the doll, sat down on the chair, and hugged her close. "That doll once belonged to our youngest daughter," Miss Anna said. "Now she's yours."

As Mary Jane rocked her new doll, gradually she relaxed. By and by, she reached into her bag and pulled out the colorful beads Miss Bet had given her as a farewell gift. She put them around her neck and sniffed back her tears. She slipped her hand into the bag once more to find the toys Wilson had made for her. *They weren't there*. Now her tears plopped onto her cheeks. In the frenzy of having to say goodbye to Miss Bet, she'd left them behind in Richmond.

Miss Anna drew her into her arms and comforted her until she was quiet. "Now let me show you around our home," she said.

Shortly thereafter, Bob and Liza bid Mary Jane goodbye and headed home to Richmond.

Mary Jane prayed every day thereafter that she would not be away from her Richmond family for long. Miss Anna spent many hours encouraging her to talk about her life with Miss Bet. She asked her what she liked to eat and let her help prepare it. On market days she made it a fun outing for the two of them. And she enrolled her in school.

Slowly, Mary Jane adjusted to living in Philadelphia with Miss Anna and her husband, and she began to feel more at home. Of course, she missed Miss Bet, Cook, and Hannah. And Wilson, too. If she thought about them for too long, tears welled up in her eyes. But her studies were easy just as Miss Bet told her they would be, and she was eager to learn.

After breakfast one morning, she surprised Miss Anna by reading to her from the newspaper. When Miss Anna complimented her on how well she read, a broad grin spread across Mary Jane's face. "I like learning to read. We read interesting things together in school."

Her first letter from Miss Bet came about three weeks after she had arrived in Philadelphia. Her insides tingled as she kissed the envelope and then carefully opened it. Her hands shook, and she wept as she read Miss Bet's words about herself, Caroline, Hannah, and Wilson. Then she told her about Harriet Tubman and her desire to help free slaves. "Miss Tubman is a former slave herself. Now she is working out an anti-slavery network to rescue others and send them North to freedom... just like I've sent you north to get an education. This network is sort of like a secret underground railroad. Miss Tubman is an official 'conductor' on that invisible railroad. Once you are educated, perhaps you will be able to help her."

Mary Jane pondered Miss Bet's words. *I don't understand what Miss Bet is telling me. How could anyone build a railroad under the ground? And if you could and it was invisible, how would you know where it was?* Mary Jane folded Miss Bet's letter, put it into her pocket and went looking for Miss Anna. She would share Miss Bet's letter and ask her to explain invisible railroads.

Every three weeks, letters brought news from home and Miss Tubman's work. Time began to move faster for Mary Jane. She read her precious mail alone in her room. The things Miss Bet told her about her black friends back home made her heart happy. When Miss Bet mentioned the snowy-white horses, her heart ached to see those beautiful animals that she loved so much.

By the time she'd been in Philadelphia for a year, she was scanning the newspapers, looking for news about Richmond. Miss Anna spent hours and hours with her from the day of her arrival, and Mary Jane began to feel at home with her and her husband. One morning at breakfast Anna said, "I'm happy that you've learned to read so well in such a short time. Would you like to read books from our family library?"

"Oh, yes, Miss Anna.''

When they finished eating, Miss Anna took her into the library. Pointing to the shelves on the right wall, she said, "The books over there are easiest to read, but you are welcome to read anything you wish."

Mary Jane perused the shelves, pulling out a book now and then, trying to decide which one to try. Finally, she settled on *Uncle Tom's Cabin* and showed it to Miss Anna. "Do you think I would like this one?" she asked.

"Yes," Miss Anna said. "Would you like to try reading it with me? We could take turns reading a page at a time."

"Oh, yes, Miss Anna. I'd like that."

"Let's sit down and begin right now." They moved over to the settee and got comfortable. "Let me read the first page. Then, you read the next one. If you decide you don't like it, you may choose a different book."

Mary Jane and Miss Anna read for about an hour. When they came to the end of a chapter, Miss Anna said, "Let's stop reading for today and talk about what we've read." And so they did. They continued this practice until they had finished reading the entire book.

Mary Jane looked at Miss Anna and spoke in a wistful voice. "I wish I could be like Miss Tubman. I'm glad she is able to help so many of our people." She paused, thinking about Miss Tubman and then said. "But I'd like to help them in a different way."

"How would you do that?" Miss Anna asked.

"I don't know how, but I would like to help bring an end to slavery in Virginia and everywhere else."

Miss Anna smiled. "That's a worthy goal, Mary Jane. Don't ever give it up. Maybe the Lord will show you how to use your gifted memory to reach it." Her comment sparked a pleasant conversation about the day Miss Bet discovered she had an unusual memory.

"Miss Bet told me I had to keep my special gift a secret from everybody until God reveals how He wants me to use it." Feeling light-hearted at that possibility, she smiled at Miss Anna. "I will pray that happens…and I'll watch for opportunities He sends my way."

By now Mary Jane's reading had improved so much that she didn't need Miss Anna's help. But through their reading and discussing the books Mary Jane read, they had developed a close relationship. Mary Jane felt comfortable living in Philadelphia. She loved going to school, and she read everything she could about slaves and slavery.

She enjoyed the letters Miss Bet wrote every three weeks, though she never mentioned coming to take her home as she had promised. As the days passed to months and then into years, Mary Jane and Miss Anna often discussed what they read in the newspapers. Mary Jane frowned the morning she read that the United States Supreme Court had ruled that blacks could never become citizens. "That's so unfair," she said.

"Yes, it is," Miss Anna said. She looked Mary Jane directly in the eye and spoke calmly. "Now that you have learned to read and process what you are reading, you can help find legal means to work against that kind of treatment of your people."

Mary Jane cringed the day she read that John Brown was hanged for his attempt to incite a slave uprising at Harper's Ferry, Virginia.

Because she could read, time passed quickly, and Mary Jane enjoyed living in Philadelphia. She was becoming an educated black woman while living in anticipation of that day when she could return home to Richmond. Ten years had passed since Miss Anna and her husband Joseph welcomed her into their home.

She was twenty-one when the best letter of all came from Miss Bet. She read it over and over and then went in search of Miss Anna. She found her in the kitchen preparing the evening meal.

"Miss Bet is coming to take me home." She made no attempt to hide her anticipation at seeing her and then going home to Church Hill. "She should arrive here tomorrow or the day after." *At last, I am going home. Home to Miss Bet. Home to Cook, and Hannah and Caroline. And to Wilson, too. I can't wait to see them again. But that means I will be leaving Miss Anna and Dr. Klapp behind. I'll have to pretend I've forgotten everything I've learned since I have been away. And I will again be treated like a second-class citizen.* She frowned and then thought of something more positive. *I've read many of the Klapps anti-slavery books since I've been living with them. Once I am home, I CAN help Miss Bet in her efforts to free my people.*

Miss Anna drew her into her arms, and they rejoiced together. That night Mary Jane was too excited to go to sleep.

Chapter Four

Daffodils, hyacinths and tulips, the most welcome harbingers of early spring, had routed the winter blues in Philadelphia. Mary Jane sat at the breakfast table, picking at her food, too excited to eat. *Today Miss Bet arrives to take me home.* She glanced at Anna Klapp. This kind woman and her doctor husband had welcomed her into their lives. They'd loved her as a daughter and encouraged her. Still, getting used to life in Philadelphia without her Richmond family had been so hard. *Sad would be a better way to describe it.*

"Will you please excuse me?" she asked.

"Of course," Miss Anna said, rising to give her a warm hug as she left the table.

Mary Jane hurried into the front room facing the street. She wanted to be there when Miss Bet arrived. Time seemed to stand still as she settled down in front of the window, hoping to catch the sound of an approaching stagecoach.

Mary Jane waited impatiently at the window as happy memories of her life before she came to Philadelphia danced through her mind. Oh, how she had missed the family she left behind. She couldn't wait to see Miss Bet and once again find Caroline and Hannah, humming as they worked together in the kitchen. And, of course, Wilson. She'd missed him, too. He was fifteen years old when she was born. She couldn't remember when he hadn't looked after her like an older brother. Many times during her first lonely months with Miss Anna, she'd reached into her apron pocket, wishing she'd find the toys he had made to cheer her.

As the days passed, she'd gradually become used to her new life. She loved going to school, and the frequent letters from Miss Bet with news of home encouraged her to do her best with her studies. But reading them had made her weep for the Church Hill family she'd had to leave behind.

Today, at last, I am going home. Still, she couldn't

ignore the tightness in her chest. *I am not that little girl who left Richmond when I was only eleven. Ten years. That's how long I've been away. Surely no one will recognize me by now. But, it's illegal for educated blacks to return home. So I am breaking the law by returning to Virginia. After enjoying so many years of speaking freely here in Philadelphia, I must play again the part on an illiterate black.* Her eyes lit up her face. *That shouldn't be difficult. Back then just one slip of my tongue would have indicated I had a photographic mind and memory. That would have been disastrous for me. But I kept my secret from everyone, including Miss Bet—until that day she heard me talking to myself.* Subconsciously she straightened her shoulders and stood taller. *I've done it before, and I can do it again.*

She shrugged away those thoughts as the three secrets she and Miss Bet held in their hearts flowed through her mind. She could never forget the day Miss Bet discovered she had a photographic memory. Or the fact that she must be cautious to keep that secret when she returned to Richmond.

Mary Jane let her breath out in a wistful sigh. Now she was returning home with Secret Number Four. *She was a free, educated black woman.* For the first time since she'd left Richmond, she began to sing, albeit softly. "Swing Low, Sweet Chariot, coming for to carry me home…"

She abruptly stopped when she spied a carriage headed toward Anna's house. Out the door, she flew and planted herself on the sidewalk to wait for the horses to stop. She held her breath as the carriage drew up in front of the Klapp home. She could scarcely contain herself as she waited for the driver to open the door and assist Miss Bet to alight.

After their long separation, cries of joy rent the air as the women rushed toward each other. Miss Bet clasped Mary Jane's hands, held her at arms' length and smiled. "You are beautiful, Mary Jane." She dropped her hands and drew her close to her heart. Tears flowed as they wept openly at finally being together again.

Mary Jane was now as tall as Miss Bet. As she looked into her face, she saw frown lines across her forehead, lines that could have been etched in there through worry. Miss Bet kissed her on her forehead and then reluctantly released her.

Once she had swallowed her tears, Mary Jane sensed that Miss Bet had not arrived alone. She turned to see who had accompanied her. "Wilson!" Her eyes locked on his, and her jaw dropped to her chest. She was not the only one who had matured during the ten years they were separated. The pleasant smile on his face showed he was looking at her differently from that day he said "goodbye" to her in Richmond. At that moment, she felt like crickets were hopping about in her stomach.

Wilson held her gaze for what seemed a long time. Then he flashed a gigantic smile and wrapped her in an intimate but discreet embrace that gave her warm feelings inside. He dropped his arms and stepped back as though embarrassed at his behavior. "It's good ta see ya, Miss Mary Jane."

Brief, as it was, she sensed he was anticipating a new and different relationship with her. He was no longer that "big brother" who ten years ago watched after her each day. Her heart rejoiced at the remembrance of how playfully he'd tugged at her cornrow braids when she was growing up. Overwhelmed by what she was feeling, she turned away from him. He no longer thinks of me as a little girl who needs his protection. *But what is he thinking?*

Wilson had called her "Miss Mary Jane," and he'd gazed at her as though she were a precious jewel dropped in his pathway, a gem that he was unworthy of picking up. *But why should he feel that way about me?* She didn't know why, and it was hard to figure it out while her pulse was thundering in her ears.

Miss Bet interrupted her thoughts. "I've brought something for you, Mary Jane." She smiled as she handed her an up-to-date Certificate of Freedom. "I doubt anyone in Richmond will remember you," she said. "But keep this with you to show you are a free black should you ever be questioned when you are alone in the streets."

She turned to the driver of the carriage. After reminding him to return to take them back to the depot to meet the early morning train, she dismissed him with her thanks and turned to Mary Jane. "We're taking the Richmond, Fredericksburg, & Potomac Railroad home. The first leg of our journey will take us to Baltimore," she said. "We'll board another train there that will carry us to Washington. From there we must go by steamboat to Aquia Creek. And then we'll board one last train that will take us on to Richmond."

Never having ridden on a train, Mary Jane struggled to mentally digest this four-stage journey that would carry her to her beloved home on Church Hill.

"I'll tell you more about train travel this evening." Miss Bet's eyes twinkled. "Just three more days and you'll be back again with us forever."

Miss Bet's consoling words spoke peace to Mary Jane's heart. She nodded to Wilson and led the way inside to greet her sister Anna and Joseph.

The rest of the day blurred past Mary Jane as she dealt with the excitement of going home at last, of seeing her beloved Miss Bet after all these years, and of

Wilson's accompanying Miss Bet north to bring her home. And most of all his reaction upon seeing her and the puzzling sensation that came over her each time he looked at her. And those times seemed to multiply throughout the day and evening.

It was early evening when Miss Anna graciously showed them to their rooms. "You must be tired after such a long journey. I want you to feel rested before you return home." Turning to Mary Jane, she said in a subdued voice, "We are going to miss you, Mary Jane. It was a privilege and a joy having you as part of our family." She hugged Miss Bet and added, "I wish you and Wilson could stay longer, but I understand your need to return home to Church Hill. "You'll find a hearty breakfast waiting for you at dawn."

Mary Jane threw her arms around Miss Anna and sobbed. She was grateful for how the Klapps had received her. But she longed to go home. Though she was too overwhelmed to speak, she knew that Anna loved her. She would understand what she could not put into words.

Miss Anna held her close until she regained her composure and then gently released her. "I wish you all a good night's rest," she said as she left them.

Back in her room, Mary Jane's gratitude to finally be going home, coupled with the excitement of seeing

Miss Bet and Wilson, kept her tossing and turning for several hours. But at last, despite her topsy-turvy emotions, sleep overcame her. So much so that Miss Bet had to awaken her the next morning.

A jumble of thoughts kept Mary Jane from enjoying the delicious breakfast Miss Anna had prepared for everybody. Though it had been difficult to be separated from Miss Bet and the others back in Richmond, the kind Klapps loved her, and she'd learned to love them in return. Miss Anna had become a special friend to her, and she would miss her. But she wanted to go home. Now she must say "goodbye."

Miss Anna held her close as she'd done the day she'd welcomed her into her family. Speaking tenderly, she said, "We loved having you live with us, Mary Jane. We will miss you."

At the appointed hour the carriage arrived, and the three travelers were soon on their way to the depot. Mary Jane had never ridden a train, so she had no idea what to expect, no idea of the seating arrangement inside the cars or the jerky starts and noisy stops as the engine roared into the station and out again.

When they reached the depot, Wilson lent his arm to Miss Bet. Before she stepped up to board the train, she smiled at him and said, "We are free to sit together in the same coach until we get to the Mason-Dixon Line. Then we'll have to move to separate cars on the train." Wilson nodded knowingly.

Once Miss Bet was safely inside, he turned to assist Mary Jane. As she was boarding, she felt his hand warm and comfortable against her back. Then his presence seemed to fill the coach and an exciting warmness radiated through her body.

Miss Bet nodded to him to sit beside Mary Jane, while she planted herself across the aisle from them. He flashed her a quick "thank you" and eased himself down.

Now the two of them were sitting shoulder to shoulder, touching, and Mary Jane's insides felt tingly. She was delighted to have him there though he seemed to be sitting much closer than necessary or proper. She felt uncomfortably self-conscious. She had lived together with Miss Bet and the other house servants for eleven years. Now at twenty-one, her body and her emotions had matured. She glanced across the aisle to see if Miss Bet might be disapproving. When she caught her attention, her deep-set blue eyes were twinkling. And then she winked at her.

Though it was obvious that Miss Bet saw nothing inappropriate, a nervous, shaky feeling skidded down Mary Jane's spine. During her past two years in Philadelphia, several young men had made friendly advances toward her, but she did not involve herself with them. Miss Bet had sent her north to get an education. She was grateful, and she would not let anything distract from her studies.

When she was growing up with Miss Bet in her big house on Church Hill, she had run to Wilson whenever she was hurt or upset, and he'd calmed her fears. But she was inexperienced with the kind of attention he was giving her now. She was drawn to him, but he was much older than she was. Not knowing how to handle the disquieting feelings she was experiencing, she eased herself far enough away from him, so that their shoulders were no longer touching--and tried to focus on her future.

What she did know was that at last she was going home, and her heart overflowed with gratitude to Miss Bet for sending her north. She was grateful that she had been given the same opportunities as white children living in Philadelphia. Leaving Richmond had been for her benefit. And just as Miss Bet had told her, her ability to remember what she heard and saw made her studies easy. Now she was happy to be on her way home to Church Hill and all that was familiar to her. Home, where she belonged and where she could use what she had learned to help Miss Bet in her fight to end slavery. Her heart was singing despite her emotional exhaustion.

Her mind and body relaxed, and her eyes closed.

Her head dropped, and she fell asleep almost instantly. A couple of hours later she was awakened by a strong jolt. The train had come to an abrupt stop. Something was holding her in place. Her eyes flew open, and she looked up into the handsome face of Wilson Bowser. Glancing down, she saw that it was his strong arm around her that had kept her from pitching forward to the floor. Feeling self-conscious about the position she was in, she looked at him again, and caught her breath.

Wilson was gazing at her with the same wide-eyed warmth as he'd greeted her the day before. Only this time his deep, dark eyes twinkled brighter than she ever remembered seeing them. The hint of a smile threatened to appear at any moment.

Wildly aware of his comforting arm around her, she didn't know what to do. Time stood still. Feeling disquieted, but not wanting to move, she was the first to look away. She hoped he couldn't hear her heart thumping in her chest or sense the crickets that seemed to be jumping to the beats.

Perhaps Wilson sensed her uneasiness. At any rate, he gently released his hold, allowing her to sit up straight. Then, as if she were just awakening from an afternoon nap, he said, "I'm sorry ya was waked up by that sudden stop." And then he added in a soft, quiet voice, "I'm glad yer comin' home with us."

By this time Mary Jane's emotions were in such a muddled state, that she couldn't trust her voice. She felt that she owed him a response. Looking into his face, she half-whispered, "I'm glad, too, Wilson."

Whatever brought the train to a halt caused but a brief interruption in their travels. They were soon chugging off again to Baltimore, Washington, Aquia Creek, and, at last, Richmond where they arrived three days later.

An unprecedented high temperature of 70 degrees had coaxed the apricot trees into blossoming, and Mary Jane was welcomed home by their delightful fragrance. And also by Hannah and Caroline. They greeted her tearfully, but also with a bit of hesitation. Mary Jane sensed that they considered her one of them, yet no longer like them. They were treating her differently.

Coming home to Church Hill after ten years' absence was an answer to Mary Jane's prayers. She was no longer that tearful, frightened child who cried her heart out when she had to leave Miss Bet. Getting a formal education had equipped her to use her photographic mind to help Miss Bet in her fight to end slavery. She couldn't wait to get started.

Wilson's attitude seemed to have changed, too, during the time she was away. Now his interest in her superseded that of the sheltering big brother who had comforted her with toys he'd made when she was sad. *What lies ahead for me? What part might Wilson play in my future? Will he play any part?* She didn't know. She couldn't wait to find out.

Chapter Five

The first week Mary Jane was home from Philadelphia, she and Miss Bet spent long hours together talking about her life up north and what was currently going on in Richmond. In the evenings she visited with Caroline and Hannah, always choosing her words carefully. *These women are my best friends, and I love them. I think they know why Miss Bet sent me to live with Miss Anna. But I don't want them ever to feel inferior around me because I have been to school.*

When Mary Jane talked with them about how she had missed them and how happy she was to be home, they listened politely. But they fidgeted and exchanged anxious glances. *Why do they feel uncomfortable in my presence? They welcomed me home. Now they treat me as an outsider. My absence has built a wall between us.*

In Philadelphia, she had lived free from wearing the mask of ignorance that now bound her to hold her tongue. She bristled each time she faced condescending treatment from the local people in the street who treated all blacks as trash. *I don't fit in with my friends at home, and when I go outside it, I must feign ignorance.* She drew in a deep breath. *I am grateful to be home, and I love my family. How can I show them I still am one of them?* She grimaced. *I am here where I belong and where I am needed to do my part in this fight for freedom for my people. But I'm too cultured for the uneducated blacks. Because I am black, the white folks won't accept me.* She shrugged and held out her hands as if she were weighing the air. *I must learn to live between two worlds. To set a guard on my lips. To choose my words carefully every time I open my mouth.* She winced. *I wish I didn't have to move out of the way or speak as though I have not one shred of common sense when a white person condescends to speak with me.*

After allowing her a week to settle in, Miss Bet assigned tasks to Mary Jane and Wilson where they could work together. One morning as they were finishing breakfast, she sent Mary Jane to look for him. "Tell him to come to the kitchen," she said.

Mary Jane found him in the carriage barn. When he saw her, his coffee-brown eyes brightened, and a bright smile sneaked across his broad jaw. Her response was a smile as pleasant as his. "Miss Bet wants you to come to the kitchen now," she said. Wilson put his tools away and followed her back to the mansion.

"The weather must have been great while we were away," Miss Bet said as they sat down together. "Now the vegetable garden needs attention. "This week I'd like you and Mary Jane to get it back into shape. Then, move on to the flower beds."

"Yes, Miss Bet," Wilson said, "we'll get right ta work." He flashed Mary Jane a pleasant smile, and the two of them headed out to the garden. Before long they worked out a system whereby Mary Jane weeded on the left side of a row while Wilson pulled the weeds on the right. As they made their way down a long line of cabbages, he told her about spending several days each spring at Miss Bet's farm outside the city helping with the spring planting.

"One day while I was out there, Misty had puppies. They were cute little balls of fur, one especially. I named him Jake." As he talked, Mary Jane turned toward him and felt the warmth of his face near hers. She caught her breath. "Let me tell something that happened one morning day when Jake was out in the garden with us. He began to speak… But his voice trailed off to an inaudible whisper.

Mary Jane glanced up to see why.

Wilson shook his head but said nothing.

"What is it, Wilson? Are you ill?"

"No…." Wilson tried to say more, but his voice had lost its power.

Mary Jane jumped up and stepped over the cabbages they'd been weeding. Kneeling beside him she said, "Wilson, tell me. What's the matter?"

Wilson reached out, drew her close, and held her tight for a few minutes.

Mary Jane's heartbeats thumped against her breastbone. She didn't know whether it was from fear of what was happening to him, or because his arms were wrapped around her, but it felt like her belly was full of gyrating crickets practicing broad jumps.

Wilson drew in a long breath and gently released her. He cupped her chin in his hands. "Mary Jane," he said, "I missed ya when ya was gone. I'd have wrote ya if I knowed how."

Mary Jane winced. She had tried hard not to do or say anything to make Wilson feel inferior to her because she'd been privileged to get an education. She sensed that he felt undeserving of her attention, and that made her heart sad. *He must never feel that way about me.* She looked him in the eyes. "Wilson, you know how to do things I can't do. You have lots of common sense. You know how to grow vegetables, and you can repair broken tools. Those are important things."

She tried to hold back her tears, but she couldn't do it for long. Since she'd returned to Richmond, Wilson had gone out of his way to be kind to her every time they were together. He was considerably older than she was. She never dreamed he would ever look upon her as anything more than his "little sister." Now he stood and lifted her up beside him. With gentle hands, he drew her close and kissed her lightly on the forehead. The world seemed to stop as they gazed into each other's eyes. Then smiling at her, Wilson took her hand and said, "We'd better get back ta those cabbages."

About an hour later as they worked their way down a weedy row of carrots, Mary Jane yanked at a weed that seemed to have very deep roots. Just as she grabbed at it to jerk it loose, Wilson slipped his hand over hers and held it there. Instinctively, she tried to pull it away, but he didn't let go. Surprised, she glanced up at him and caught her breath. He had no intention of freeing her hand immediately. For a few electric moments, they locked eyes, setting those crickets off on another round of exercises in Mary Jane's stomach.

Wilson released his hand and pulled her to her feet. "Mary Jane, I missed ya when ya was away. And then…then…then when I saw ya after all these years, ya looked so growed up and purty that…"

He could not finish his sentence. Mary Jane tried to interpret what he was feeling. The crickets understood, and it threw them into a frenzy. Or were they leaping for joy? It made no difference. She had missed him and Miss Bet and everybody else in the Van Lew household. Missed him because he'd always looked after her. But now that she was home, her affection for him had deepened. Her heart had opened to him on a different plane. He meant more to her now that she had grown up.

They had worked another hour or so when again Wilson took her hand and guided her over to a bench under a majestic old cottonwood tree. "Let's sit and rest a bit," he said.

Before long, Mary Jane was telling him how much she had missed everyone. How she cried herself to sleep each night for weeks. And how hard it was being away from her family. Now sensing he cared about her in a new way, she said, "Wilson, when we were coming home from Philadelphia, it set my heart racing when I awakened from the jolt, and you were holding me."

In response to her words, Wilson reached out and

gently turned her chin so she would face him. He gazed into her eyes, as dark and bright as his own, and whispered, "You is very special ta me, Mary Jane."

As he reached out to embrace her, Mary Jane closed her eyes and leaned into his strong arms. Wilson held her close until their breathing returned to normal. Then gently releasing her, he winked and said, with reluctance, "We'd better get back ta those weeds."

From then on, each evening after they finished their work for the day, Wilson came to the mansion to talk with Mary Jane. Sometimes, they visited on the steps of the side porch, watching the fireflies in the dark shadows of the magnolias while the fragrant pink mimosas perfumed the night air.

Other times, they spent the evening in the drawing room, growing together emotionally, voicing their love for each other. Whether outside or in, they dreamed of being together forever. Though Miss Bet had given them their freedom years ago, still no one outside Miss Bet's household knew. Mary Jane reminded Wilson that they must continue to be careful that no one found that out.

Mary Jane had been home from Philadelphia for three weeks when Miss Bet invited Wilson to have breakfast with her and Mary Jane. As he entered her mansion, the delectable smell of pork and dried corn wafting out of the kitchen whetted his appetite. Mary

Jane's dark eyes sparkled when she saw him. "Miss Bet remembered that's our favorite breakfast," she said.

Miss Bet invited them to sit down at the breakfast table. Shortly afterward, Caroline appeared with a steaming platter of hog 'n hominy.

"Thank you, Hannah," Wilson said. Turning to Miss Bet, he said with a big grin, "You remember what we both like, don't ya, Miss Bet?"

Miss Bet nodded in return. "You two have been doing a super job with the garden work, and I appreciate that." Her approval of their work and her obvious pleasure at seeing them develop a close relationship was evident in her words. But it appeared she had something else on her mind.

Once they'd finished their meal and laid down their forks, Miss Bet turned to Mary Jane and said, "I've not been sitting around on my hands these years you've been away. Now, that you are home, I can turn some of my work over to you." She shifted her weight and sat back in her chair, her posture ramrod straight as always. She inhaled a deep breath as though savoring the moment. Then, wearing a confident grin, she said, "Together you and Wilson can do something I've been attempting. I had to give it up because people were suspecting my motives."

Speaking with delight in her voice, she said,

"Wilson, the vegetable garden and the flower beds look wonderful. But since we were away for nearly a week, the shrubbery and the lawn look neglected. I want you to spend your mornings catching up on these yard duties." She turned to Mary Jane. "I'm sure you can keep the vegetables and the flowers looking cared for from now on."

She paused long enough to allow Caroline to clear the table and then began anew. "Because Richmond has such a large black population, it's difficult for local authorities to spot runaways on the move. And that attracts more of these men, and occasionally women, fleeing from their cruel masters." She rubbed her brow as if to ward off a headache. "These runaways must keep an eye out for slave catchers sent by their owners to search for them, and also for local whites who might lie and claim they own them so they can sell them at auction."

Miss Bet focused on a butterfly outside the kitchen window. "Wilson and I've done our best to help them, but it's slow-going work." She exhaled then looked up expectantly. "Now that you are home, I've drawn up a new plan to help more of these fleeing slaves get to freedom in Pennsylvania."

At the mention of a new plan, Wilson grabbed Mary Jane's hand, and her heart began to beat fast in expectation. Miss Bet's plans were always unique, challenging, and tested before she put them into practice. "I will help our people any way I can," Mary Jane said.

Wilson nodded. "You know I will, too." he said. Mary Jane trusted Miss Bet's wisdom and her experience, and she knew Wilson did, too. "So what are your plans, Miss Bet?"

"Yes, please tell us. How can we help you?" Mary Jane added.

Miss Bet drew in a big breath and let it out with a sigh. She started slowly, but her voice grew more excited as she laid out her plans. "I've kept alert to announcements of runaways in the *Richmond Daily Dispatch* and watched for posted broadsides with descriptions of the blacks on the run. I'd picture in my mind what they looked like. Then Wilson and I wandered about the streets trying to spot them, but we had to be careful not to draw attention to ourselves."

She stopped and snatched a breath of air. "We rarely found them. They stayed away from public view as much as possible." Her voice died out as she paused and stared into space as though making a mental count. "I think we rescued twenty men and hid them until I could send them safely north to freedom." She paused again and huffed out some air. "The problem was getting them to the hidey-holes without raising suspicions…or drawing attention to where they were." She turned to Mary Jane. That's where you and Wilson fit in."

Mary Jane's eyebrows squished together. "Hidey-holes? What are they?"

Miss Bet tried to cover her smile with her hand. Mary Jane cast a quick glance at Wilson. He wore that same look on his face, but he wasn't trying to hide it.

"Mary Jane, do you remember the day you helped me take food upstairs to a black man who was hiding in my attic?"

"So that's a hidey-hole?"

"No," Miss Bet said, "though it served the same purpose. But hidey-holes are places in Richmond where runaways can be safe when passing through as they make their way North. If they sense they are being pursued, they can slip into one and be hidden from sight very quickly." Miss Bet settled into her chair more comfortably. "It's likely those men that I hid and then sent north spent a night or two in a hidey-hole before they learned to come up to Church Hill to get my help."

"Oh," Mary Jane said. "Now I understand."

Miss Bet picked up where she had left off earlier in the conversation. "While you were away, Wilson and I did everything we could to help the black community. Your people understand my motives are pure, and they put their trust in me. Together we set up several secret places where runaways can hide until they can continue on their flight to freedom." A broad expectant grin covered Miss Bet's face. "Most every black man in Richmond can lead a runaway to a hidey-hole."

Wilson sat up bit straighter and asked, "How does Mary Jane fit into your plans?"

"She can read the newspapers with me looking for ads about fleeing slaves. By the time an advertisement appears in the press, the trail of an escaped slave is often lost. But not always. These men love their families, and they risk getting caught when they sneak home to see them." Miss Bet paused as though she were thinking of the fate of men caught on the run. "I want you to wander around the streets watching for pictures posted of runaways. Should you spot any of these people, take them to the nearest hidey-hole."

Miss Bet tapped her right temple with her index finger and continued. "In the beginning I want you to wander about near the slave jails in the Shockhoe area for a couple of hours in the afternoons. If you see auction signs, check the dates and the names and descriptions of those up for sale." She paused. "If I recognize any of them as spouses of freed slaves, I'll buy them on auction day."

Mary Jane and Wilson exchanged knowing glances. Miss Bet would free them as soon as she could draw up their papers and send them north to be with their spouses.

"Always take your marketing sack with you, Mary Jane. And one more reminder. You'll need to look as though you are on an errand so don't dally long in one spot."

Mary Jane wasn't sure she understood Miss Bet's intentions for them. "So you want us to go down the hill to Shockhoe every day and just wander around?"

"Not every day. I don't want people down there getting used to seeing you. Some days I'll send you to the market instead, supposedly on an errand for me. You'll need to make an occasional purchase to put into your sack. That way you're less apt to arouse suspicion."

Mary Jane was grateful that finally she could do something tangible to help her people. She was willing to do anything she could to rescue runaways. The fact that Miss Bet was sending Wilson with her would give them lots of time to nurture their love into full bloom.

Chapter Six

The mid-summer sun was shining brightly when Mary Jane picked up her sack as she and Wilson prepared to go down to the market. "I'm glad you remembered to take that with you," Miss Bet said with a grin. "Anyone who sees it will assume you are on an errand for your mistress."

Mary Jane nodded. "It helps me fit in with the other servants in the streets."

As they walked along, Wilson elbowed Mary Jane, and they stepped to the curbside of the street as two white shoppers approached them. "Because we're blacks, iffen we step aside and stay out of their way, we're not worth the white man's attention."

Mary Jane winced at his accurate observation as they meandered through sections where they might find broadsides offering rewards for runaways. Often the dates were posted for slave auctions with descriptions of the unfortunate blacks being up for sale.

They'd wandered for about fifteen minutes when Wilson nudged Mary Jane. "They's one of 'em broadsides," he whispered."

They edged over until they were close enough for her to read it. Mary Jane needed but one sharp glance to remember the descriptions. Speaking loud enough for only Wilson to hear, she read aloud the description of a young man named Jim. "He's about 19 and has a scar across his forehead."

"Let's check the hidey-holes first ta see if he might already have found one of them," Wilson said, pointing Mary Jane in the direction of the hideaway just a few blocks away. "If we finds Jim there, I'll talk with him, so he knows he kin trust us. Once he accepts our help, ya tell him about the secret room. Then ya can go home and alert Miss Bet that I'm bringing him home afta dark."

Mary Jane paused to process this plan in her mind. It was almost clear except for one thing. "Wilson, how will Miss Bet know it's you knocking at her door?"

"Do ya remember the man ya saw hiding in the attic when ya helped Miss Bet carry food up ta her secret room? He was one of many she has helped ta run away ta freedom. These men know which door ta approach and about the secret knock." He reached out and took her hand. "This is it: Tap-Tap. Tap-Tap-Tap. Tap-Tap." If ever ya hear that knock, you'll know it's someone on the run, needin' Miss Bet's help."

Together they headed to the nearest hidey-hole. It was empty. So was the second one. But at the third one, Mary Jane and Wilson recognized Jim by his scar. Wilson approached him slowly and then called out in a hoarse whisper, "Jim, my name's Wilson. Have ya heard of Miss Bet? I've come ta take ya ta her. She'll arrange for ya ta go north to freedom."

At the mention of Miss Bet, Jim slipped out into the open. "I knows who Miz Bet is," he said. "I'se glad ya found me…and I sure does thank ya."

Wilson reached out with a friendly hand and then introduced Jim to Mary Jane. She greeted him graciously. "Once you get ta Miss Bet's mansion on Church Hill, she'll keep you hidden in her secret room," she said. "She'll take care of you until she's worked out a way for you ta get out of Richmond." She looked him in the eye and assured him that he could trust Miss Bet and that she had been helping men like him escape to freedom for many years. "You need to use a special knock when you get to Miss Bet's home. That way she knows you need a hiding place right away."

"I'll go git ya some food for today," Wilson said. "When I return, I'll teach ya that secret knock and explain how ta find Miss Bet's house, jist in case we should git separated on our way up Church Hill."

"Thank you, Miz Mary Jane, for helpin' me," Jim said.

When Mary Jane turned to say goodbye to Wilson, he pulled her close. "Please be careful on yur way home."

"You must be careful, too," she whispered as she hesitantly took her leave and headed back to Church Hill with her market sack.

As she trudged along, she envisioned Wilson, returning with food for Jim and himself. He'd spend the rest of the day comforting him. When darkness descended on the city, he'd guide him up Church Hill where Miss Bet would be waiting for them. She would not rest until Wilson and Jim arrived home that night by cover of darkness.

Three days later, Jim was on his way to freedom.

The next evening when Mary Jane and Wilson were together, they talked about Jim. "I'm glad we found him before he got caught and sent to auction," she said. Her voice trailed off, and Wilson looked at her to see why. When he saw tears pooling in her eyes, he took her hand and held it until she could continue.

She looked directly into Wilson's face. "I saw an auction when I was a little girl. Miss Bet had taken me with her on an errand. I don't know why she didn't pull me away from it sooner." Mary Jane shuddered at the memory. "I dreamed about that auction for many nights after that. The evil carried out that day against my black brother is imprinted on my mind. I hate seeing our people forced to grovel to their cruel masters and so does Miss Bet." She looked at Wilson and said, "I'm glad she sends us on rescue missions searching for runaways. I want to be like her, to do what I can to set our people free."

Wilson nodded and squeezed her hand. "It's good we kin work together, helping rescue them one by one."

During the next few months, Wilson and Mary Jane made regular forays throughout Richmond and into the Shockhoe area, searching for fleeing men. Mary Jane would hurry home from her "market trip" with Wilson to report to Miss Bet. Miss Bet always thanked them whenever they directed a new "guest" to her door.

"It's our way of thanking ya for our freedom," Wilson said.

"And for the kind way you have always treated us,"

Mary Jane added.

October weather turned drizzly, and their searches dwindled. But working together to help their "brothers and sisters" had enabled them to spend time with each other almost daily. At the same time, the love relationship that began the day she left Miss Anna's home in Philadelphia blossomed. Mary Jane was happy to be home, happy to be helping her black friends, and happy to have fallen in love with Wilson Bowser.

However, while they had been busy looking for runaways, the determination of the majority of the people in Richmond to keep blacks in subjection had become more pronounced. Still, they took heart the morning Mary Jane read in the newspaper that Abraham Lincoln had been elected President of the United States. Miss Bet and all her freed servants rejoiced together. Their hopes for a better tomorrow for all blacks were rekindled. But not for long. About six weeks later, South Carolina seceded from the Union.

Chapter Seven

The successful rescues that Mary Jane and Wilson carried out brought great joy to their hearts. And simply being together was an added blessing. Day by day, the warm, protective feelings Wilson showered on Mary Jane grew into a relationship far beyond mere friendship. Despite the difference in their ages, they had fallen deeply in love with one another.

By now Mississippi, Florida, Alabama, Georgia, Louisiana, and Texas had joined South Carolina in seceding from the United States. In February 1861, they formed the Confederate States of America and chose

Mississippian Jefferson Davis as their president. The happy couple had no way of knowing what that portended for their people still enslaved, but they would pray for a just outcome as they faced the future together.

One March evening when Wilson was visiting Mary Jane and Miss Bet in the drawing room, Miss Bet excused herself and went for a walk. Though it was not unusual for her to allow them to spend time alone, Mary Jane sensed that Wilson had something on his mind. They had grown to know more about each other the past few months. But that night, he seemed unsettled. As the door closed behind Miss Bet, he eased himself nearer to her. When she felt his protective arm around her drawing her close, she relaxed against his shoulder. But not for long.

Wilson pulled back a short distance from her and caught her eye. "I have something for ya." He reached behind his back and retrieved a small wrapped package. "Mary Jane, I missed ya after ya left us ta go-ta Philadelphia." He handed her the box. "This helped me to remember ya."

Mary Jane's looked at him wide-eyed as she received his gift. *What could I possibly have left behind to remind him of me?* Because it was from him, she knew she would treasure it. At that very moment, those gyrating critters showed up again in her stomach. She loved Wilson. She was pleased that he wanted to gift her. But she was grateful the raucous little songsters kept the sounds of their serenade inside.

Her hands shook as she unwrapped the package and carefully opened the box. When she saw what was inside, the floodgates in her eyes broke open. Wilson enclosed her in his muscular arms holding her close to his heart and wept with her.

Eventually, their tears ceased. Wilson swallowed and kissed her softly on both cheeks until calmness returned to both of them.

As Mary Jane stared at the three items in the box, her mind flew back to her childhood days. First, she picked up her little worn-out-by-love corncob doll and focused on it. "You made this doll for me when my momma died." She placed it lovingly back inside the box. Next, she picked up a little moon winder made from two walnut shells. "You made this the day I fell down the cellar steps and broke my leg." She held it a few minutes before returning it to its place.

When she picked up the last item, fat tears plopped onto her cheeks. "You made this top for me that terrible Sunday when Miss Bet took me to St. John's church to be baptized." She swallowed trying to control her emotions. "I was so scared that morning." Her lips quivered. She looked at Wilson, too overcome to say more. Wilson comforted her in the warmth of his strong arms. When she was able to speak, she said, "These precious things somehow got left behind when I went to Philadelphia."

Wilson held her close giving her time to process her childhood memories. Bye and bye he said, "I missed ya so much, Mary Jane. Every night ya was gone I looked at the things ya loved. I knowed you'd miss them." He swallowed and went on. "Ya was so afraid ta leave Miss Bet." He gently smoothed her cheeks with the palms of his hands and then ran them through her hair.

Mary Jane took a deep breath and whispered, "I looked and looked for them. I cried when I couldn't find them at Miss Anna's." She focused her teary eyes on Wilson, while searching for the adequate words to express her appreciation. "Keeping these things for me was the nicest thing you could have done." She swallowed and dried her eyes. By and by the sparkle returned to them. She looked into Wilson's face. "What can I do to show you how happy you've made me by saving my childhood treasures?"

Wilson studied her face for what seemed a long time. Then looking at her through the eyes of love, he whispered, "Mary Jane, will ya please teach me how ta read?"

Mary Jane snuggled close to him and whispered in

his ear. "Of course, I will."

Wilson wrapped her in his arms tighter than ever before. "I loves ya, Mary Jane. Will ya marry me?"

Mary Jane looked into his face, blinked, whispered, "Yes," and cuddled close to his heart.

When they shared with Miss Bet their commitment to marry, she gathered them into her arms and wept. "Today you've made my heart glad," she said.

Despite the threatening war clouds, Miss Bet promised to plan a wedding for them at none other than St. John's Episcopal Church. Though it was rare, they would not be the first black couple to marry at St. John's. Miss Bet could not conceal the motherly love she felt toward them. She took them by the hand and promised, "I will leave no stone unturned to make your wedding day a memorable occasion for the entire Van Lew household."

But fate intervened on April 12 when the Confederate Army opened fire on Fort Sumter, the almost completed federal garrison on a man-made island in South Carolina's Charleston Harbor. The War Between the States had begun. Nevertheless, Mary Jane and Wilson Bowser were married in a joyful ceremony at St. John's Episcopal Church four days later.

The day after their wedding their home state of Virginia seceded from the Union and joined the

Confederate States of America. Jefferson Davis immediately ordered regiments to report to Richmond. While the newlyweds were spending their first days together as man and wife, militia companies from the Confederate states poured into the city. Camp Lee was set up at the Fairgrounds on West Broad Street to accommodate them. About 200 uniformed cadets from Virginia Military Institute arrived to teach the men the art of soldiering. The people of Richmond welcomed the men with martial music, and martial boasts filled the newspapers.

Two days after Virginia's secession, President Abraham Lincoln issued a Proclamation of Blockade against Southern ports, limiting the ability of the South to stay well supplied to fight against the North. The effects of that blockade would be far-reaching no doubt. But for now, Mary Jane and Wilson were too enamored with one another to consider what it portended…and the cherry trees blossomed into full bloom as if to applaud their marriage.

For a brief time, the newlyweds were able to put aside the forecasts of doom and destruction that would devastate the beautiful city of Richmond and tear them apart in the process. But, soon the slow leak of reality set in and the impending conflict over the right for anyone to own another had to be reckoned with.

Chapter Eight

In June, Mary Jane and Wilson moved from Church Hill to the Van Lew vegetable farm a quarter of a mile below the city, near Harrison's Landing. "Wilson, I want you to supervise their work," Miss Bet said. "Many of the vegetables planted in February and March are ready to be harvested, and the farm is short-handed."

Mary Jane and Wilson exchanged quick glances. They'd enjoy getting away from the noisy city…and having time to be alone. Two days later they moved into their cottage. Now, with more time for themselves, Mary

Jane continued to teach Wilson to read.

About six weeks after they'd settled into their new home, Mary Jane received a note from Miss Bet inviting her to come home to Church Hill for tea. She beamed as she read the brief letter. She would enjoy spending time with Miss Bet, but she wondered if she had some new idea to discuss. *Was the invitation an excuse to get her to come back into the city?*

A pleasant tingling warmed her heart a few days later as Miss Bet welcomed her with a wide smile. "First we'll enjoy our tea, and then we'll talk," she said, leading her into the parlor.

Hannah entered shortly after that with a tray laden with the tea set and a plate filled with fresh pastries. Mary Jane recognized the fine china, and her eyes opened wide. And then she saw the silver. Lying beside the dainty cups were two Paul Revere teaspoons. Miss Bet used them only on very special occasions. *Why is Miss Bet treating me with such honor?*

Mary Jane's heart began to pump faster as she searched her mind for possible reasons for this tea party. *Did Miss Bet have some bad news to share? Was she ill? Was she going to leave Richmond to live with Miss Anna in Philadelphia?*

Hannah poured a little milk into Miss Bet's cup and then added the steaming tea. Mary Jane held her cup still while she did the same for her. Then she gently swished her spoon back and forth, being careful not to the touch the sides.

Miss Bet nodded toward the tempting pastries on the tea table. Mary Jane helped herself to a lemon tart but remained seated on the edge of her chair.

"I've missed you," Miss Bet said. "I can see that you and Wilson are enjoying your new life together."

A broad smile spread across Mary Jane's face. "Yes, Miss Bet. Thanks to you, we are. We love being alone, away from the city, and now I have more time to teach Wilson to read. But I've missed you, too." She picked up her tea, took a sip, and stared hard at her adoptive mother. "Thank you for inviting me to take tea with you again."

Miss Bet nodded as though she were following their conversation. But rather than responding to Mary Jane's comment, she inhaled a deep breath and blurted out, "I've found a new way to help our side win this war." Speaking in a calmer voice, she said, "Much has happened since I sent you and Wilson to the farm, Mary Jane. I've been visiting the Union soldiers in Ligon's Prison. These poor men were captured at that fierce battle at Manassas." Her voice cracked, and she swallowed. "I pay attention to what is going on around me like someone else I know. I listen for information that might be useful to our Northern generals." She took another sip of tea and then continued. "Once the war officially began, I organized an underground network for gathering information. Now I spend much of my time spying for the North."

"You are a spy?" Mary Jane's heart leaped inside her chest. She gulped, almost spilling her tea. Her hand shook so much that she set her cup down before that happened. To be sure Miss Bet had done some risky things through the years, but spying? What if she got caught? Knowing the penalty for spying, she gasped.

Her heart thumped as Miss Bet talked about her spying activities, but they also aroused her curiosity. Not wanting to miss a word, she leaned closer.

"Our Northern men who were brought from the battlefields as prisoners kept their eyes and ears open along the way. They listened to the guards talking among themselves, and they remembered conversations with doctors and occasional Southern deserters. When I visit them, they tell me what they've heard. By fitting their bits and pieces together, I gather information that sounds useful to our Northern generals. I pass it on through my underground network."

As Miss Bet continued to explain how her spy ring operated, their tea cooled, and the pastries were forgotten. She raised her right hand with her fingers spread wide. "I have set up five points along the James River to deliver information to Major General John E. Wool at Fort Monroe. A courier in my network takes the information to one of those points. A second one carries it across the river to a waiting steamboat that delivers it to the fort."

Mary Jane couldn't keep still. "Miss Bet, why are you telling me this?"

Miss Bet waved off her question and stared into space, frowning. "What I pass on is useful, *I think*. But our generals need more. They need to know specific attack plans in time to prepare for a defense. Or even an advanced attack." A puzzled expression creased her brow. "I must expand my network to ferret out when and where the South intends to attack next. And how many men they will have in their line of march. That kind of information will prepare our generals for each battle."

Mary Jane's thoughts were racing through her head. *Once Miss Beth hatches an idea, she barrels her way through until she's worked out the details. Sometimes through normal channels. Sometimes through hair-raising adventures. And often through cunning and courage.* What does she want from me? *No one in Richmond knows I can read and remember everything I see and hear. Does she think there's some way I can help?* Mary Jane's hands began to sweat.

Miss Bet resettled herself in her chair and spoke in a no-nonsense voice. "Everyone who loves justice must support the Union until we win this war. I will sacrifice everything I have to bring that about." She inhaled and exhaled loudly. "If we could find out the enemy's plans before they attack, we could warn our troops in time to meet them head-on."

Mary Jane nodded, willing herself to stay calm. *Miss Bet is a thinker. A schemer. And daring. What she is planning is certain to be outlandish. Just where is this conversation heading?* She edged forward on her seat. "How can you find out the plans for attack before they are set in motion?"

A hint of a smile creased the corners of Miss Bet's mouth. "Varina Davis, the wife of Jefferson Davis, the President of the Confederacy, is one of my friends. She needs more servants in the Confederate White House. Right now she's looking for someone to help with the housework and the care of her three children with another on the way." She pursed her lips and tapped her cheek with an index finger. "What a fabulous opportunity! By acting dull, thick-headed and submissive, an alert housemaid could gather firsthand knowledge to pass on to me." Miss Bet tapped her foot, a sure sign of eagerness to get on with her plan. "I *must* find someone to work for Mrs. Davis as a housemaid and for me as a spy."

Mary Jane knew Miss Bet well enough to surmise where this conversation was heading. She fought to make herself sit still. Having been brought up by Miss Bet, she had adopted some of her cunning and courageous ways at an early age. *Becoming Mrs. Davis' house servant might enable me to help the North win the war and help put an end to slavery. Miss Bet freed all of her slaves. Now that I have tasted freedom, I want all of my people to be free.*

As Miss Bet poured out her plans, a sly grin spread across her face. "Once the new servant learns the routines and customs of the White House, she will have access to the President's office. That's the first step in my long-range planning. As soon as I find someone who can pay attention to what she sees and hears and remember it, I will recommend her to Mrs. Davis." She took a long sip of her cool tea, set her cup back on the table, and raised an eyebrow expectantly.

"So you expect this new servant to read President Davis's confidential war plans as she cleans his office and straightens his desk?"

A sheepish grin etched its way across Miss Bet's face. "That's my goal."

"Supposing she gathered some important information? How would she get it to you?"

"In my underground network, I have couriers *in* uniform and *out*—here in Richmond and the North. We already have in place channels for funneling information to our northern generals." Miss Bet dabbed her mouth with her napkin. "A member of my underground lives across the street from the Confederate White House. She's ready to help transfer any information she receives."

Tiny drops of sweat peppered Mary Jane's forehead. Her heart raced. *Spying on President Davis in the Confederate White House sounds daring and dangerous.* She leaned forward in her chair as Miss Bet continued.

"Thomas McNiven, the local baker, is a link in my underground network. My White House plant could pass on battle information to him when he makes his scheduled deliveries to Mrs. Davis." Miss Bet stopped for breath and then added, "I'm putting in place details for other plans as well. Plans that could be more effective, but with *greater* risks. For now, I must find a smart woman to help, and she must be fearless."

Miss Bet paused, took a deep breath and locked her eyes onto Mary Jane's.

Mary Jane owed so much to Miss Bet, and she heard the longing in Miss Bet's voice. She could not keep silent. "I could do that," she blurted, "…if Wilson approved."

Miss Bet nodded, knowingly. She laid a gentle hand on Mary Jane's knee. Speaking in a soft, affectionate tone, she said, "I'm sure you could, Mary Jane, but before you commit yourself, think about the price you must pay if you accept. You are naturally intelligent, and you have been blessed with an unusual memory. Now that you have received a formal education, do you want to sacrifice all that and continue to wear that mask of ignorance around others?"

Miss Bet paused long enough for Mary Jane to weigh her words, and then continued. "Actress that you are by nature, you'd have no problem pretending to be as witless as most whites think all black folks are. Of course, your unusual memory would be an asset." She chuckled. "Since you are a woman of color, the President, and his guests would pay no more attention to you than they do to the chairs on which they sit." Miss Bet palmed her chin with one hand and spoke somberly. "But...you'd have to leave Wilson and move into the servants' quarters. Are you willing to sacrifice the loving relationship you share with him?"

As Mary Jane pondered these things, Miss Bet stared at nothing for a minute or two. A shadow seemed to have crossed her face. "If Mrs. Davis or anyone else discovered the truth about you, I shudder to think of what might happen. You could be beaten. Worse yet, it might cost you your life."

Mary Jane's dark eyes widened, but she kept silent.

"The risks are grave." Miss Bet reached out, enfolded Mary Jane's hands in hers and looked into her face. "The penalty for spying is death...by hanging."

Mary Jane stiffened in her chair. She tilted her head from side to side weighing what she might accomplish against the consequences of being discovered.

Do I want to leave Wilson to do this? To live in the White House as a deceiver? To be bossed around like a dull servant? Is it worth risking my freedom? Or my life? Will Wilson permit me to do it?

Her heartbeats hammered inside her head. She closed her eyes and thought of her precious husband. Being separated from him would be the hardest thing she had ever faced. She loved him dearly, and his love for her was just as strong. *What will he think about me risking my life?*

After a few minutes, she opened her eyes and looked at Miss Bet. "I understand the risks," she whispered. "If Wilson gives me permission, I'll accept them—for you. And for my people."

And if I fail? She forced that thought from her mind.

Chapter Nine

Later that evening back home at the farm, Mary Jane sat on the steps of their little cottage breathing in the sweet-scented balsam nearby. It was a peaceful scene, but her country was not at peace. Neither was her heart as she pondered how to share with Wilson what Miss Bet proposed. *How will he feel when I tell him I want to become a spy for her in the Confederate White House?*

For the twentieth time, she replayed in her mind what Miss Bet had told her about the underground network. The risks were great, more so for her than for a well-to-do white woman like Miss Bet. But that wasn't what bothered her most.

Since Wilson had grown up in the Van Lew household, Mary Jane knew he was familiar with her fierce determination to see slavery brought to an end. Now that they were enjoying every minute they spent together as husband and wife, she knew he'd be alarmed at the thought of their living apart, and she didn't like that idea either. *He'll be upset when I tell him I'll be risking my life by spying on President Davis.* Finally, she mustered her courage, took a deep breath, and set off to talk with him.

She found him inside in his favorite chair, petting their hound dog Jake. "Wilson?" she said, seating herself on the arm of his chair.

He looked up and caressed her face with his eyes.

"We need to talk. About my visit with Miss Bet."

Wilson turned and looked straight at her, concern showing in his eyes. "Mary Jane," he said, reaching for her hand, "What's troubling ya?"

Mary Jane hesitated and then spoke haltingly, struggling to keep her potential involvement under control. "Wilson, I'm grateful that Miss Bet sent me north to be educated." She took time to choose her words carefully. "Few of us blacks have that opportunity. Since I benefited so much by being freed and educated through her generosity, I want to show her how much I appreciate what she has done for me." She took a deep breath. "Wilson, she needs my help. How can I say 'No?'"

Wilson's breath quickened. "What will ya do?"

"She wants me to join the spy network she has set up to help the Northern armies."

Wilson leaped to his feet. "A spy? She wants ya ta be a spy?" He grabbed a breath of air. "I loves ya, Mary Jane. I cain't let ya put your life in danger like that."

Mary Jane cupped his face in her hands and looked directly into his face. "Wilson, she gave you and me our freedom. She risks her life daily to help all our people. How can I refuse to help?"

Fear clouded Wilson's eyes. "W—well just what would ya be doing in her spy ring?"

Despite her efforts to hide her enthusiasm, Mary Jane's words tumbled out, and her voice shook. "She wants to hire me out as a servant in the Confederate White House. To spy on President Davis."

Wilson shuddered and turned away. "Be a spy in the White House. Surely, ya don't want ta do that."

"Yes, I do."

"No, Mary Jane. If ya got caught, ya would be hanged on the gallows at Camp Lee. I loves ya. I cain't let ya risk your life like that."

"This is how I can show Miss Bet my appreciation for setting me free and then caring for me like a mother."

"I don't like that idea one bit."

"Wilson, I'm aware of the risks." She lowered her voice. "The threat of death by hanging terrifies me enough to guard my lips and my behavior." She inhaled deeply through her nose and then exhaled through her mouth. "Miss Bet already has one spy connected with the Confederate White House. It's the baker, Thomas McNiven. Thomas lives about one mile from the White House. He's often out and about in Richmond after he finishes his daily deliveries. Thomas has influence with the people of Richmond on both sides of the slavery issue. If ever he found me in a tight spot, Miss Bet says he could get me out of it."

"Mary Jane, I knows I'm not as smart as ya are. But I knows about a lot of things that ya don't. Spying right under their noses is too dangerous. I cain't let ya do it."

"I want to do what I can to make things better for our people. Not just spend my days pretending to be an illiterate slave in Miss Bet's mansion."

Wilson shook his head. "I missed ya like crazy when ya wuz up north gettin' educated. I cain't bear the thought of ya leavin' me...or riskin' your life for Miss Bet."

"It's not for Miss Bet, Wilson. It's for all our people." She hauled in a big breath and continued trying to make him understand. "Somebody must be willing to take risks. Or do you prefer that we lose the war? That our people remain slaves forever?"

Wilson held his head between his hands. "Of course I want us ta win the war."

Mary Jane curled her hands into tight fists. *He doesn't understand how much I would be able to help.* "Wilson, this is more important than our happiness." She blinked and faced him with fierce determination brightening her eyes. "Somebody must get this information from the White House. Don't you think I could do that?" She reached out and put her arms around his neck. "My precious husband," she whispered, "I learned early on to keep my eyes and ears open and my mouth shut."

Wilson raised his head and looked long into her face. Then he wrapped his arms around her once more in a fierce hug. "Mary Jane, "I loves ya too much ever ta be separated from ya again."

Mary Jane drew in another deep breath, closed her eyes, dropped her head, and exhaled.

The next day as they were finishing their lunch, the rattle of wagon wheels interrupted their conversation. Wilson went to the door to see who was coming. "It's Miss Bet," he said. "She's all in a lather and wearin' her get-out-of-my-way-I-have-work-ta-do face."

Mary Jane joined him in the doorway as Miss Bet

climbed down from the wagon. She was breathing hard as she greeted them. Mary Jane grabbed a rag to wipe down the sweating horse before walking him to cool him down. Meanwhile, Wilson brought him a bucket of water.

"What did ya do, Miss Bet?" Wilson asked. "Gallop out here the whole three miles from Church Hill?"

Miss Bet gulped in some air and then blurted out her news. "Thomas McNiven has brought me some information that must be delivered to Fort Monroe as quickly as possible." She turned directly to Wilson. "Tonight he's blocked from passing information. It's up to me and my network to get it there."

She drew in a few more deep breaths and wiped the perspiration from her face with a lace handkerchief. "Wilson, you've always been a faithful servant. Now, I'm asking you for a really big favor. I wouldn't ask, if it wasn't important." She drew her shoulders up, tucked her elbows into her sides and looked long into his face. "Would you be willing to carry a message down river to Harrison's Landing tonight—if I explained how to do it?"

Mary Jane gasped. *Miss Bet wants Wilson to become part of her spy network. To risk his life, delivering a secret message. He's probably never done anything secretive in his life.*

"To Harrison's Landing?" Wilson's eyes widened, and he stroked his jaw with his left hand. "Isn't that about six miles from here?"

Miss Bet nodded. "Yes, Wilson. It is…."

Wilson frowned. "Just how do ya 'spect me ta get to Harrison's Landing, Miss Bet? That's 'bout two hours by foot if ya knows where you're a goin'. More at night and maybe dodgin' lookouts."

"I'll tell you." She took a deep breath and began. "First of all, you won't be walking, Wilson. You'll go by water. Fortunately, at this time of the year, the moon is pale. Push yourself off in a rowboat down the creek to the river. Once you get there, you can rest your arms a bit and let the natural current carry you toward the landing. When you come to the Union gunboat patrol, hold up your hands. To show you're unarmed."

"Then what?"

"Explain that you are delivering a note from a Richmond source. That it must reach Fort Monroe as quickly as possible."

"Won't Confederate patrol boats be on thuh river? What if one of them stops me?"

Miss Bet bit her lip. "That could happen. You'll need some excuse for being out there at night." She paused for a minute. "Tell them you're taking medicine to your ailing mother down river. Then be sure to have some herbs or something with you." She stared hard at him and then added, "You'd have to guard this message with your life, Wilson. It must not fall into enemy hands."

She reached into her bag and pulled out a pair of heavy shoes with double soles. She picked one up to show Wilson the hollow inside. "One of my helpers is a Richmond cobbler. He's making these brogans for my couriers, so they can hide messages inside them." She glanced at Wilson's feet and back to the shoes. "It looks like they should fit." She hesitated and then added, "It's good to have these shoes. Otherwise, the only safe place to carry the message is inside your drawers."

Mary Jane lowered her head at Miss Bet's comment. But she was most concerned with Wilson's response. *I wish I knew what he is thinking. Do I dare ask him not to risk his life?*

"Beggin' your pardon, Miss Bet. But wouldn't a patrol think it strange iffen he saw I wuz wearin' new brogans? Wouldn't it be better ta scuff them up some so's they looks worn?"

"That's good thinking, Wilson. You'd need to do something to make them look old." Miss Bet looked at him and then at Mary Jane. "You are both special to me, and I don't want you getting hurt." She paused, and then added, "But I have no one else who can deliver this message tonight. If I did, I'd not ask you to risk your life."

Risk my life? Wilson gazed at Mary Jane with questioning eyes.

Mary Jane drew in a deep breath. *How can I refuse to let him risk his life for the cause of freedom when I want him to do the same for me?*

Mary Jane hesitated momentarily and then nodded ever so slightly to Wilson.

Wilson squeezed her hand and turned to Miss Bet. "Ya freed me and my precious Mary Jane years ago. I will do this fer ya and fer my people who are still owned by others.

Miss Bet thanked him and embraced Mary Jane. She reached into her pocket and pulled out a small paper that was folded small enough to fit into the shoe easily. She handed it to Wilson. "General McClellan will be pleased to receive this information. Thank you for seeing that he gets it."

Wilson picked up one of the shoes and poked the note inside the double sole.

"Thank you, Wilson. I wish you Godspeed." Miss Bet turned to leave. "Now I must get back to Church Hill to make my afternoon visits to our prisoners."

Though she'd agreed with Wilson's decision to deliver Miss Bet's message, Mary Jane worried about him. She hunched her shoulders and fisted her hands to keep them still.

Wilson interrupted her thoughts. "I gotta git to the field," he said. "The others will wonder what's keepin' me from showin' up." Mary Jane walked with him to the door and kissed him. The coming night would be a long one.

Chapter Ten

Mary Jane sewed the last stitch in the hole in Wilson's trousers' pocket and handed them to him. Then she sat down on the bed to watch him prepare for his trip down river to Harrison's Landing.

Wilson curled his fingers around the slender package of bitter herbs for his "ailing" mother and put them in one of his pockets. "I'm ready ta go, Mary Jane."

Darkness was slowly descending on their cottage. Whippoorwills called to one another and several night critters scurried out of their path as they walked hand-in-hand out to the tree-lined creek beyond the potato patch.

The pale moon shining through the trees cast a shimmering reflection on the gently rippling water.

Wilson hugged Mary Jane, kissed her on both cheeks, and lowered himself into a borrowed rowboat and grabbed the oars. "I'll be back as soon as I can," he promised as he pushed off from the dock. The oars creaked in their rowlocks and plopped into the water.

Mary Jane stood bravely waving until he disappeared around a bend in the creek. *Please be careful, Wilson.* She turned and trudged back to the cottage, trying to ignore the images of what-might-happen-to-him flashing across her mind.

When she opened the door, Jake roused, stretched, and came to her, wagging his pleasure in seeing her. Then he looked around as if to say, "Where's the master?"

She reached down and stroked the dog's head. "Don't worry, Jake. Wilson will be back," she said, as much as to assure herself as the old hound.

That evening the dog shadowed her every movement, offering his comforting presence. When she finally settled down enough to go to bed, he nuzzled her hand, heaved a sigh, and dropped to the floor beside her.

Mary Jane tossed and turned for hours willing her mind to be at ease. *Miss Bet's plans always work out by and by. I have no cause to worry.* Time seemed almost to stand still until she drifted into a restless, unsatisfying sleep.

Shortly before dawn, the sound of heavy footsteps jolted her awake. Her pulse quickened. *Who? What?* She wondered as she shook off her sleep. Jake shuffled over to the door, wagged, and whined.

Wilson was home. Mary Jane sprang from her bed and flung open the door. Her exhausted husband clung to the railing. She rushed to help him over the threshold. "I'm glad you're back. I worried about you all night long."

Wilson leaned against her warm shoulder, dragged himself inside, and collapsed onto their bed. Mary Jane plied him with questions. "Did everything go as planned? Did you get stopped? Did you have any trouble?"

Wilson looked at her through half closed eyes, too weary to respond.

Mary Jane removed his heavy shoes, pulled off his socks, and curled up beside him. She would let him sleep as long as he needed to. And then they would talk.

When he awakened about three hours later, Mary Jane slipped out of bed to prepare breakfast. He joined her shortly and encircled her in a tender hug.

"I never 'spected Miss Bet ta ask me for help," he said as Mary Jane beat the eggs. "I'm glad I could deliver that message. I cain't believe she trusted me with something that important." He paused. "I stayed in the shadows as much as I could. I thought I was 'bout halfway ta the landing when the moon come out from behind the clouds. That's when I spotted a gunboat ahead of me. I couldn't tell if it was ours or Rebels."

Mary Jane's heart skipped a beat. *Rebels could have captured Wilson.*

"I didn't 'spect a Confederate vessel ta be so close to Harrison's Landing. I ran my speech about my sick mother through my mind. In case I needed it." He sniffed the cheesy grits and scrambled eggs. "You know what I likes best for breakfast."

Mary Jane looked at him with a demure smile. "Thank goodness I mended that hole in your pocket. I shudder to think of your being caught without those bitter herbs."

"'Wish I could say the same for the hole in Abe's boat," Wilson said. "It had a small leak. If it had been any bigger, it would have swamped me for sure."

"Oh, dear me. What a fright."

"I grabbed up my oars so I could go faster and closed the distance between us as quick as I could 'til I saw it was a Union patrol."

Mary Jane chuckled. "So you didn't need that medicine for your ailing mother after all."

Wilson grinned. "No, but I had it jist in case." He flexed his shoulders and rubbed his neck. "When I wuz close enough for them ta see me, I held up my hands. Jist like Miss Bet told me ta do. The patrol boat drew up beside me. 'I've a message fer General McClellan,'" I said. "I sat down and took off my shoe ta git it."

Jake nudged him for attention, and Wilson paused to give him a pat. "You know how small that message was. Well, jist as I was handing it ta one of the patrolmen who had questioned me, a wave blew up. My boat lurched. The message flipped into the air and…"

Mary Jane dropped her spoon. "NO."

"…And landed back into my hand. My heart was thumpin' inside my chest. I'd nearly lost the message. Botched my mission. My hand shook when I gave it ta 'em." He lowered his voice. "Both hands shook a long time after that."

Mary Jane set the meal on the table and kissed the top of his head. "I've married a brave man."

"Not brave, Mary Jane. But happy to do Miss Bet the favor and wantin' ta get home safe ta you. I turned the boat and started rowin' up the river. I was goin' against the current, and I still needed ta keep hidden. By the time I got back ta the creek, my arms felt too numb ta pull anymore." He winked at her and added, "But I thought of ya and kept on rowin'. I didn't take a full breath until I wuz back on our porch."

"I don't know how I could have survived if something had happ...."

Wilson stroked his chin. "It's a good feeling knowin' I did something ta help the Union." Then he added with an impish grin, "I'd do it again...iffen my wife would let me."

Mary Jane hugged him and whispered into his ear. "I'm sure she would." Seeing this as an opportunity to plead her case, she added. "Now you understand why I want to help Miss Bet."

"Women don't belong in war, Mary Jane. "Spyin' is men's work."

Mary Jane tensed at his words. "But men can win this war faster with the aid of smart women like Miss Bet...and me."

She studied Wilson's face willing him to see that she had a God-given ability that could help Miss Bet gather crucial information from the Confederate White House.

"Wilson, is there another colored woman in Richmond who can read and write? Another who has been educated in the North? Another one who understands and remembers everything she hears and sees?"

Wilson looked into her eyes, but he couldn't keep a

straight face. "No. No. No, I bet there's no other woman, colored or white, with a memory like yours." Now he was almost grinning. "With your skills, you *could* gather the kind of information Miss Bets wants from right under President Davis's nose."

Mary Jane's grin spread across her face. "So, it's okay to accept Miss Bet's offer to hire me out as a servant in the Confederate White House?"

"Yes," Wilson said, as he drew her close once more. "I loves ya enough ta give ya my blessing ta do what ya wants most." He lowered his voice and whispered in her ear. "It's going ta be mighty lonely at the farm without ya." He swallowed and then murmured, "I hope this war don't last forever."

"So do I," Mary Jane whispered under her breath.

Chapter Eleven

Mary Jane stood on the porch the next morning and watched Wilson amble toward the vegetable gardens. Then she went inside to write a brief note to Miss Bet:

> *Miss Bet,*
> *Mrs. Bowser gratefully accepts your*
> *kind invitation to tea.*

She reread her note, slipped it into her pocket, and headed outdoors. An empty wagon nearby waited to be loaded with the fresh cauliflower, kale, and other fall vegetables, as well as eggs, to take to Richmond. Later in the day, a servant would come out from the city and swap his empty wagon for the full one.

Mary Jane made sure that she was alone before slipping her note under the wagon seat. Miss Bet always checked the wagons for messages from her underground members.

A few days later, Miss Bet visited Mary Jane again. Mary Jane welcomed her with open arms. They were soon seated around her kitchen table catching up with the latest news over their tea. Knowing how persistent her friend was in working out her well-organized plans, Mary Jane felt certain that she'd contacted Varina Davis already. She was bursting to find out if that happened A hodgepodge of muddled feelings tumbled through her mind. Her heart pounded. She tried to ignore it, but that was difficult.

Miss Bet set her teacup back on the table, and Mary Jane scooted a little closer. Now she waited wide-eyed to hear what she had worked out. Miss Bet rarely wasted her time with idle conversation.

"Yesterday, I called on Varina Davis in the Confederate White House. After she shared in some small talk, I told her I'd read her advertisement in the *Dispatch* for a housemaid."

Mary Jane stiffened. Miss Bet's preplanning was

paying off.

"I have made arrangements for you to meet Mrs. Davis next week."

Mary Jane laughed nervously as Miss Bet continued. "Once you get to the White House, you'll need to get acquainted with President Davis, Varina, and their children as quickly as possible. You must win their trust. Getting Varina to accept you as a reliable member of her staff will pave the way to weave yourself into the White House routines. And to set things up to help you gather the kind of information we need."

She paused, and then added, "You'll need to be patient, Mary Jane. During this time you'll be my sleeper agent until you hear what you recognize as classified information to pass on to me. That's when you'll spring into action."

Miss Bet chuckled. "I worked hard to keep a straight face when I said you were a hardworking girl, though not terribly bright. I told her you worked well in the dining room and parlor."

Mary Jane sniggered. "At least you said I know how to serve."

Miss Bet nodded. "Now, let's get serious. My friend, Eliza Carrington, lives across the street from the White House. Her seamstress visits on a regular basis. Varina sends her gowns for mending regularly." A satisfied look crossed Miss Bet's face. "Fortunately for us, that seamstress is a member of my underground. Once Varina trusts you, she'll send you with her torn gowns to Eliza. When the seamstress knows the day and the hour to expect the mending, Eliza will let me know. I'll visit her soon after that to pick up any information you have for me."

Mary Jane chewed her lip as she processed Miss Bet's plans. Slowly a frown creased her brow. "What if I have information that needs to reach you immediately and it's not time for the seamstress to visit? How will I get the information to you?"

"That could happen, Mary Jane. If it does, hang a red shirt on the laundry line. When I see the shirt, just before dusk, I will meander into the area close enough for you to find me. If for some reason you can't slip out at dusk, give the message to Thomas the next morning." She glanced at the clock over the fireplace. "I must get back to Church Hill. Today is my day to visit our men in Ligon's prison. As soon as I can, I will visit Eliza and set up a time for you to meet her seamstress."

She lowered her voice. "In the meantime, you need to start thinking and acting dimwitted. God forbid that your secret is ever discovered."

In a flash, her expression changed. "I'm asking so much of you...and Wilson. These last days while I work

out my plans, love him with every inch of your being."
Then she added, almost under her breath, "Once you
make the move, the White House could be your home as
long as this war lasts."

Mary Jane nodded her understanding. Wilson had
risked his life to do what only he could for the sake of
the Union. She was willing to do the same.

A week later, she and Miss Bet walked the twelve
blocks down Church Hill to the Confederate White
House on the corner of Twelfth and Clay Streets. Mary
Jane gasped when she recognized the spreading roofs of
the Shockoe Valley stretched out below them. A chill
crept over her as the memories of the slave market she'd
seen there many years ago flashed across her mind.

About fifteen minutes later Varina Davis opened the
heavy oak door to the mansion and welcomed Miss Bet.
She greeted Mary Jane politely and asked her a few
questions before accepting her as a house servant.
Speaking as though Mary Jane were not present, she
turned to Miss Bet and said "I will have a room prepared
for her immediately in the servants' quarters. Bring her
back to me tomorrow."

Miss Bet shook her head. "Not tomorrow, Varina,"
she said. "She is a good worker. I'll need her help for
another week before I give her up."

Mrs. Davis drew in a deep breath and released it

before speaking. She raised her chin and said, "Well then, I will expect to see you and the girl in one week."

Mary Jane stood by silently, staring at her feet.

One morning a week later as Mary Jane approached the Confederate White House with Miss Bet, her heart beat so fiercely she could scarcely speak. Her steps slowed the closer she got to her uncertain future.

A house servant answered their knock and led them to a small reception room where Varina Davis welcomed them and bid them sit down. Mary Jane breathed deeply to quiet her nerves. Sensing Mrs. Davis's eyes on her, she stood until she was told to take a seat. Then she took the nearest chair, folded her hands in her lap, and kept her eyes low as Mrs. Davis talked briefly with them. Then as if on cue, the house servant returned. Mrs. Davis nodded in her direction. Rising, she said, "Mary Jane, Martha will show you to the servants' quarters."

"This way, please." Martha led them down a narrow hallway to the kitchen and out a back door to a humble building standing alone a short distance from the other servants' quarters. "Mistress Davis wants you to live here," she said, "so you will be close to the kitchen." Mary Jane's heart lightened when she saw a small glass window near the door. What a pleasant, unexpected luxury!

Martha lifted the latch, and the two of them stepped

inside a small, snug room. Mary Jane noted the door latched from the inside. A colorful braided rug lay next to the bed. Directly across from the door stood a nightstand with one drawer and a small table and chair. To the right of the door were several pegs where she could hang her clothing. Though austere, it looked more comfortable than most quarters where her colored friends lived.

Mary Jane closed her eyes briefly. In preparation for her new job, she had been acting slow-witted as she had done with Miss Bet ever since Mrs. Davis hired her. Now, as she considered this new challenge, she felt a pleasant tingling in her chest as she returned to the White House with Martha. She concealed her thumping heart and hid the warm affection she felt for Miss Bet as they said their goodbyes.

Mary Jane adapted quickly to her new position. Each morning she paused quietly outside the kitchen door and drew in a deep breath. Then she straightened her apron and headrag and prayed. *Please, Lord, don't let me betray myself.* She slipped inside the mansion through the servants' door, closing it quietly behind her.

"Good-mornin', Mistress Davis," she said, keeping

her head down. Varina Davis acknowledged her with a nod, and Mary Jane set to work helping prepare hog and hominy left over from the previous day as breakfast for the family. It was important that she avoid eye contact with Marse and Mistress as much as possible, lest she appeared to be an uppity servant.

She had become one in a small group of house servants, free blacks, and immigrants who took care of the Davis family and the daily operations of the mansion. Most of them were friendly to her and day by day she developed a closer friendship with several. Each had specific assignments from Mrs. Davis which left little time for anything but their work, and that helped her keep her identity a secret. In just a few days she noted that not all were loyal to the Davises. Every morning she overheard William Jackson, the President's servant and coachman, praying for Marse's defeat.

From the first day she served as a housemaid, Mary Jane stayed alert for war information. While preparing meals, caring for the children, or feather-dusting the home, she listened carefully, storing in her memory what she heard. As best she could, she kept aware of President Davis's whereabouts when he was at home. He ignored her completely. One day he nearly clearly collided with her when she was carrying an armload of laundry. Apparently, he had greater concerns on his mind than a new servant in the household.

On her second day at work, she had overheard him, saying that although the South had won the battle at Manassas, it was at the cost of 2000 men. "This war is *not* going to be over in just six weeks," he lamented. A few days later Mrs. Davis gave her a new job.

"This afternoon I want you to dust the President's office and his private reception room. Tomorrow he has guests coming for dinner." She paused and then added, "Mary Jane, you are doing your work well. I am pleased. I know I can trust you with more important duties. I want you to serve them."

Mary Jane's heart quickened. "Yes, Mistress," she replied, grabbing the feather duster.

As she attacked the dust particles on the President's desk, she glanced at his dispatches. Struggling to keep her expression bland to hide her excitement, Mary Jane read through them with ease. They were confidential messages meant for President Davis's eyes alone. One of them stated that the Confederate government faced a severe labor shortage. To make up for it, they planned to force free black people into the army against their will. She noted names and locations to pass on to Miss Bet.

A second letter revealed revolt within President Davis's Cabinet. His Secretary of War, LeRoy Pope Walker, was planning to resign because he thought the

President lacked the ability to make wise decisions. Furthermore, he didn't seem to distinguish between what was important and what was not. And also, he refused to take advice from his military advisors.

Mary Jane completed her afternoon duties and scurried off to hang the red shirt on the clothesline to alert Miss Bet that she had news. Before returning to her quarters, she recorded what she had read and hid the notes in the hollowed-out heel of one of her shoes.

As was her habit, Miss Bet meandered into the area just before dusk. She'd be careful not to be seen from the White House, yet linger near enough that Mary Jane could find her.

This evening was the first time Mary Jane would deliver a message outside the White House. As she considered what lay ahead, her heart pounded in her ears. She would be leaving her quarters after the evening meal and must return before dark. Slaves were forbidden to be alone in the streets after curfew. If she were caught once the sun had gone down, she would be beaten, or worse, sold at auction.

She wished she were back home on the farm with Wilson. *I hope it won't be too long before I see him again.* She closed her eyes long enough for a brief prayer for protection. She had volunteered to join Miss Bet's underground network. She *would* deliver that message to

Miss Bet. Fear caused mistakes. Mistakes caused discovery. Discovery meant death. No matter what, she dared not give in to fear.

Chapter Twelve

Once Mary Jane served the evening meal and cleaned the kitchen, she was free until breakfast time. She returned to her servant's quarters, checked to make sure the message was still in her heel, and waited for nightfall. As soon as she deemed it safe, she inhaled deeply to calm her anxious feelings, grabbed a light wrap, and slipped outside.

The war had changed Richmond. Camp Lee was set up within the city. And the long brick Virginia State Armory, east of Tredegar Iron Works, had become the Confederate States Armory.

Shortly after that, the five railroads that served Richmond arrived loaded with soldiers from every region of Virginia and every state of the South. The camp soon contained 25,000 troops who immediately began drilling for battle.

Tobacco and cotton were no longer Virginia's main products. Now that the war had begun, while it continued to build locomotives, the Tredegar Factory also produced siege guns and field pieces, artillery shell, and armor for ironclad gunboats, as well as machinery for making other weapons.

Mary Jane knew well the rules her people were forced to accept when in the streets. Being outside alone without a permit was forbidden. So was being out at night after curfew. Simply going out at all in the evening made her a target. She must take all precautions possible to become invisible.

She slipped out of her quarters and looked both ways to make sure no one was in sight. She did not wish to encounter the hoard of prostitutes, gamblers, and other ne'er-do-wells who followed the soldiers into Richmond, crowding the streets and making it dangerous for any women they encountered.

Just ahead of her in the next block, a small cluster of men and women were headed west toward Seventeenth Street. *Good.* Since that was the direction she needed to go, she followed them staying close enough to appear that she was with them.

Just before she reached the railroad tracks, she spotted Miss Bet, standing in the shadow of a tobacco warehouse. She hurried to greet her.

"You must have learned something about troop movements," Miss Bet said.

Mary Jane pulled the folded message from her shoe and handed it to her. "It's not about troops or attack plans," she said. "But it seemed like something you'd want to pass on."

Miss Bet nodded and tucked the note inside her sleeve. "Thank you."

Before she could say more, the alarm bell rang out from the brick guard tower: two loud strokes, a pause, and then a third stroke. Mary Jane's heart leaped at the first clang. Again and again, the bell rang. What should we do?"

"The bells are calling out the militia to report to the square," Miss Bet said. "The men will be pouring from their homes as soon as they grab their arms and supplies." She glanced around and said, "You'd better avoid the main streets. You will be safer if you take the long way home. Follow along the railroad tracks to Leigh Street. That's five blocks from your quarters." She gave her a quick hug. "I'm sure you can find your way,

Mary Jane. I'll be praying for you."

Mary Jane darted off toward the railroad, wishing her feet could move faster. The rattling of their gear, the clank of canteens, and the pounding of boots against the cobblestones amidst the shouting of the men assembling for duty spurred her on. Soon the heavy tread of armed men filled the air followed by the hustle and bustle of more militiamen assembling on Broad Street.

Thank goodness I'm heading in the opposite direction. But I've never taken this street, and it doesn't have gas lights. If it weren't so dark, it would be easier to see where I'm going.

As she scurried as fast as she darted down the unfamiliar street, her foot struck something soft. *What was that? It felt like an animal. Was it dead or alive? Was it dangerous?* She stopped in her tracks and then backed off. Peering down, she relaxed. It was a small opossum…and it seemed as frightened as she felt.

The brief stop enabled her to catch her breath. She stepped around the animal and sped on. Two blocks from Leigh Street she spied another animal, crossing the railroad tracks just ahead of her. Not an opossum. This critter had a wide white stripe down its back.

Unlike her, the skunk was in no hurry. Mary Jane stopped to give it a clear path. She'd never be able to explain it if the skunk sprayed her. Once it moseyed off the other side, she ran as fast as her breathing would allow until she was safely back inside her quarters. First mission accomplished. She sank onto her bed and murmured a prayer of thanksgiving.

The next morning when Mary Jane slipped into the kitchen, Bessie, the head cook, greeted her warmly. "As soon as we finish breakfast, I'll show you how to set the table for Massa's dinner guests," she said. "Then I'll explain how to serve each course of the meal." She looked her up and down and added, "I'm sure you can do it, and do it right, once I tell you how it should be done."

"Thank you, Bessie," Mary Jane said. About an hour later the two of them headed to the dining room, and Bessie kept her promise. Once she had explained everything clearly, Mary Jane set the table exactly as she'd been told. "You've done well, Mary Jane," Bessie said as Mary Jane put the last piece of silverware in its place. "Now let me show you how to serve the food. Don't worry about getting things mixed up. I'll be in the kitchen making sure each course is ready in turn."

Mary Jane thanked Bessie, and they returned to the kitchen and began the dinner preparations. Now several hours later, the time to serve the meal had arrived. Mary Jane's nerves were jangling. The steaming oysters she carried in the tureen sloshed wildly, threatening to plop over the side. What if an oyster landed in the President's lap? Or in the lap of one of the three generals who were his guests?

She leaned against the doorjamb of the dining room and held her breath. Today she'd be serving dinner to President Davis and the visiting generals for the first time. *One, two, three...* She counted in her head to calm her nerves.

If anyone finds out my secret mission, I will be...

She drew in a deep breath and held it. *Thank you, Lord, that Mistress Davis trusts me to serve the President. Please don't let me call attention to myself.*

Clutching the hot bowl, she nudged open the door with her right foot and slipped into the dining room. With each shaky breath, her shoulders heaved. Her stomach roiled like the sloshing oysters. She struggled to calm the sea of soup and keep the waves of broth from splashing out onto the fine linen tablecloth. If she embarrassed the president, Mistress Davis would send her packing, and that would be the end of her career as a spy.

Inside the dining room, three uniformed men sat around the rectangular oak table engaged in a lively conversation with President Davis. As they explained their troop strategy and movements to him, not one of them glanced her way.

Mary Jane ladled out the first serving of the bubbling stew into the President's bowl without fault and moved on to the first guest, a dignified general of medium height. In contrast to his receding hairline, his full grey beard flowed down his chin to his chest. *How does he find his mouth behind all of those whiskers?*

Splash. Several plump oysters plopped into his bowl.

Mary Jane gasped.

The general didn't seem to notice. He accepted his portion as though it had been doled out by disembodied hands. Looking directly at the President, he said, "I'm grateful that we won that first confrontation at Fort Sumter." He spooned an oyster into his mouth. "Since there were no casualties on either side, I thought this would be a quick war." He paused as if measuring each word before it left his lips. "After what happened at Manassas, it's obvious that I was wrong."

Mary Jane served each guest in turn and escaped to the kitchen where she promptly forgot everything she had just heard. *Calm down and focus,* she berated herself. Determined to listen, she returned with the salads.

"…when we get those troops across the river," said "Gray Beard."

President Davis addressed him as General Lee.

"Where will you make your next move?"

Lee nodded toward another guest with a long, dark, full beard. "General Stuart can tell you that."

As Mary Jane placed General Stuart's salad in front of him, a whiff of cologne caught her by surprise. So did the red flower in his lapel. Struggling to hide her amusement, she missed the general's first response. She must not miss anything else said around the table.

"Tell him about our plans for the bridge," the third general said.

"We'll destroy it. Then the Union will have to ford the river or go around to make their counter-attack," General Stuart added.

The President turned to the third guest. "How will you be supporting him, General Beauregard?"

"My troops will be on the march before daybreak Tuesday at the same hour Stuart's men move out."

Mary Jane served the guests roast chicken and then gumbo while noting every detail of the discussion. She distributed the chocolate ice cream she had churned earlier that morning and returned to the kitchen with calmer nerves, steady hands, and a head full of details about the Confederate plans for the Tuesday attack on the North. This information was important. It needed to reach the Union as soon as possible.

She filled the dishpan, grabbed the soap, and set to

work. Her first time to serve President Davis and his guests had gone smoothly. Moving machine-like at her task, she formed her plans to get this information to Miss Bet that evening. First, she must hang that red shirt on the clothesline. As she was tidying up after the midday meal, Mrs. Davis came to the kitchen. "I'm pleased with your work, Mary Jane," she said. "I thought you could serve well, and you did. Now I have a gift for you." She handed her a hair switch.

Mary Jane gasped. Fake curls were a luxury that black servants would never own. *What does she expect me to do with that? Shall I wear it when scrubbing the pots and pan? Or perhaps while dusting the parlors. Still, it's a gesture of appreciation, and it was probably the best she dared offer under the circumstances.*

"We use these to keep our hair up," she added as if Mary Jane wouldn't know that.

Mary Jane curtsied. "Thank yuh, Mistress." *A pair of shoes...or a comb would have been more useful.* Nevertheless, Mrs. Davis had complimented her on her work, and she couldn't wait to share the information she'd overheard with Miss Bet.

She finished her day's chores by straightening up the children's room and glanced at the clock. Though the sun was lowering in the west, it wouldn't set for another two hours. Still, she had no idea how long it would take to find Miss Bet. She needed to be on her way. In the interest of time, she decided not to go back to her quarters first.

Instead, she tiptoed down the basement steps and peered out the cellar door. After two days of unusually high temperatures, there was a sultry stillness in the air, and those who were in the street appeared intent on finding a cool spot. A hasty glance up and down the hill assured her that Twelfth and Clay Street were sparsely populated. She crossed to an even less traveled street that would take her toward Miss Bet's Church Hill mansion. Occasionally she cast a furtive glance over her shoulder to assure herself she was not followed.

As she crept along, she stayed close to the buildings now shadowed by the setting sun. To reassure herself she patted the hair switch in her pocket as she walked along. As peculiar as the gift was, it proved one thing. Mrs. Davis was satisfied with her work.

Just before she reached the railroad tracks, she spied an old woman shuffling along muttering to herself. The soles of her worn out slippers slapped the ground as she ambled down the dusty street. Mary Jane recognized her profile and quickened her pace until she caught up with her. Then the two melted into the shadows behind a large building.

Once out of sight, Mary Jane giggled

uncontrollably. "You look like an escapee from the insane asylum. Where did you find that ugly dress? And buckskin leggings?" She clutched her sides to keep them from bursting.

Miss Bet joined in the laughter. "Just wait until you hear me sing…off key."

"Why are you dressed like that?"

Abruptly Miss Bet's laughter stopped. "One morning as I headed to Ligon's Prison, I met Varina Davis on Clay Street. When she saw I was carrying food to the prisoners, she scolded me." Miss Bet mimicked her former friend. "There are sick and hungry men in every house in Richmond. You're crazy to feed our enemies." Her eyes snapped shut, and she clutched her hands in a death grip. "I shrugged my shoulders and continued on my way. Varina and I used to be friends. Since the day she saw me taking food to the prisoners, she has not been friendly."

She stared at her palms and pursed her lips. "Now she rarely acknowledges my presence. When she sees me in the street, she looks away. Nobody pays much attention to me. As I continue to visit our prisoners, more people scowl when they see me. So I've begun disguising myself." She laughed aloud. "Sometimes I wear cotton bonnets and calico dresses in the streets. And sometimes I act insane. That's how I overhear things. Important things." She glanced around. "You must have learned something about troop movements? What news do you have for me tonight?"

Mary Jane knelt in the dust and pulled a tiny folded paper from the hollowed-out heel of her right shoe and handed it to her. "Here's what this bumbling, tongue-tied, illiterate servant read yesterday in a dispatch on President Davis's desk. It's not about troops or attack plans," she said. "But it seemed like something you'd want to pass on." She handed Miss Bet a second piece of paper. "This is what the President and his generals discussed at dinner today."

"Good work." Miss Bet tucked the notes under the frayed bonnet that hid her tangled blond curls. Thank you."

Mary Jane pulled the hair switch from her pocket. "Yesterday Mistress Davis gave me a gift. 'We wear it to hold our hair up,'" she said, mimicking Varina Davis.

"Wonderful, Mary Jane. That's shows that she has accepted you."

"Yes, but does she think I am blind as well as thick-headed?"

Miss Bet chuckled softly. "I hope so," she said, squeezing Mary Jane's hand. Then she added, "You don't want to know what she thinks." Her voice softened. "I knew you'd earn her trust in time. Now, go quickly," she whispered.

The two parted as furtively as they had met.

Mary charged off in the direction of the White House. She was about halfway home when she heard barking dogs off in the distance. Were they chasing a runaway slave? *Dogs trained to track runaways by scent are vicious beasts.* Visions of what might happen if the poor man or woman got caught flashed through her mind. The noise of the chase grew louder as they neared. She shuddered and ran faster. She must stay in the shadows a much as possible while being careful where she was going.

The frenzied barking reached a fever pitch. As she stopped to catch her breath, she heard a scuffle and then a piercing scream. The dogs had caught the fugitive.

Paralyzed with fright, Mary Jane pressed her body against a tall building. Her heart ached for the poor victim, but there was nothing she could do to help. Fear put wings to her feet, and she sped the last few blocks to safety in her quarters. She was relieved to be home at last, but she couldn't stop thinking about the unfortunate runaway caught by the vicious dogs.

Right then, Mary Jane made a solemn vow to herself. She was in this war for the long haul. She would work with Miss Bet and her underground to network in every way possible until they won it and broke the bonds of slavery that held her people captive and at the mercy of their cruel white masters. She was as wedded to this cause as she was to Wilson—*'til death do us part.*

It would take hours for her breathing and her heartbeats to return to normal.

Chapter Thirteen

Though inside she was grinning, Mary Jane put on a neutral face early one summer morning when Mrs. Davis sent her on an errand. The war was in its second year, and the once peaceful city had become an armed camp with troops pouring in. Since many freed blacks worked for wealthy slave owners, she was not apt to be singled out for questioning as she headed to the *Dispatch* office with Mrs. Davis's message. She slipped in amidst the people milling around the bulletin board outside and, using her photographic memory, "copied" the latest news.

Mrs. Davis had been sending her out frequently since supplies of food and other necessities normally available were getting harder to find. Mary Jane used each errand to check the bulletin board. She had read a few days earlier that a series of battles fought along the swampy Chickahominy River just east of the city had lasted for seven days. General Lee eventually thwarted General McClellan's Union forces' attempting to capture the city. But the cost was a tremendous loss of lives on both sides. Now seven days of high temperatures and much soaking rain had created an atmosphere of gloom. Mary Jane watched through bleary eyes as a long, steady procession of horse-drawn ambulances, wagons, and oxcarts carrying the wounded and the deceased clogged the streets of Richmond.

One afternoon as she helped serve tea to Mrs. Davis and several invited friends, she overheard them lamenting what was happening throughout their city. "What a pity the hospitals are turning the ambulances away," one woman commented.

"They lack space, soap, bandages, drugs, and everything else needed to care for the wounded men brought to their door," another said as she set down her cup of tea, now made of chicory and acorns. "They have no alternative."

Mary Jane cringed. Not even the White House was

immune to scarcities of things ordinarily taken for granted. In her effort to do help the Confederate States of America, Mrs. Davis had given up much of her silverware to make bullets. She taught her children to share the only spoon she'd kept for them.

Whenever she was in the streets for any reason, she noted that many private homes, schools, hotels, and warehouses were now hospitals for the wounded. But still, more and more casualties were carried into the city. She could not hold back her tears the first time she witnessed a frustrated driver, dumping his wounded in the street and, she supposed, hurrying back to the battlefield to pick up others.

Mrs. Davis sighed. "Setting up tents throughout the city gives the men shelter…" She paused as her voice quivered. Once she was able to go on, she added in a disconsolate voice, "Even so there are not enough nurses or medical supplies to care for them." She blinked several times and added, "God bless those weary nurses who wash and reuse the bandages made from our good linens and petticoats."

When she was no longer needed to help serve the guests, Mary Jane retreated to the kitchen. Then she slipped off to a private place to deal with the horrible scenes, flashing like lightning, flooding her mind: scenes of wounded soldiers dying in the streets while awaiting medical treatment. Added to the repugnance that pervaded the atmosphere was the stench of bodies yet unburied for lack of enough gravediggers to take care of them. Meanwhile, the flies enjoyed a heyday. People hesitated to go outside. When they had to do so, they covered their noses and mouths and tried not to breathe the abhorrent air.

One morning when Mrs. Davis sent Mary Jane out, she noticed a larger-than-usual number of people around the *Dispatch* office, reading the latest news. She edged her way close enough to read the posting. Her heart sank when she read the number of casualties:

> 20,000 CASUALTIES IN LEE'S
> NORTHERN ARMY OF VIRGINIA
> 3,500 KILLED
> 15,750 WOUNDED
> 950 CAPTURED OR MISSING
> 16,000 CASUALTIES IN THE UNION
> ARMY
> 1,735 KILLED 8,000 WOUNDED
> 6,000 WOUNDED OR MISSING

Mary Jane choked back her tears. *How can Richmond possibly handle all the wounded...or the prisoners?*

She thought of Wilson. *At least, he has Jake to keep*

him company through the long, lonely nights. "Stop it." she admonished herself inwardly. "You must put him out of your mind lest someone notices, and you betray yourself."

Back inside the White House the other house servant girls nodded or smiled when they crossed paths, but none of them had time or energy for small talk about the war or anything else. William Jackson, the President's servant and coachman, had always greeted her with warmth should they happen to meet, but she hadn't seen him for several days. She wondered if he might be ill.

It was just as well that she didn't become too friendly with the other girls since she had to hide her feelings along with her identity. Privately she mourned the thousands of soldiers on both sides who were killed in battles, as well as the wounded ones and the men brought to Richmond on prison trains.

Whenever her duties necessitated going outside, she covered her ears. She hated the piercing sounds that now polluted the air. Shrieking train whistles signaled the arrival of more wounded Confederate soldiers, Union prisoners, and corpses. Mounted cavalry tramped the streets sounding like herds of wild cattle amidst artillery fire piercing the air. Bugles blew reveille, waking babies and adults from their sleep.

The sweet scent of drying tobacco had given way to the putrid odor of rotting flesh. And the acrid smell of gunpowder made the air even more offensive. Mary Jane stuck cotton into her ears and tied a scarf around her mouth and nose to avoid these horrors of war.

Beautiful, peaceful, bounteous Richmond had become a riotous, ugly city where one could not breathe easily, find adequate food, or even purchase necessities at reasonable prices.

One afternoon, Mary Jane completed her routine work much sooner than usual. "I am excusing you until it's time for your late evening duties," Mistress Davis said.

"Thank you, ma'am."

Mary Jane welcomed the unexpected time off. After tucking her pass into her apron pocket, she slipped away to visit Miss Bet. By now, the city was cursed with overcrowding from the living and the dead. Fumes from burning tar barrels polluted the air, yet their billowing clouds did little to cover the wretched stench of death and dying.

Halfway up toward Church Hill, she was nearly overcome by something so putrid that she grabbed her stomach and threw up her lunch. Off to the left stood an old farm wagon piled high with rotting corpses. Mary Jane charged up the cobblestone street to Church Hill as fast as her weakened legs could carry her.

Miss Bet herself opened the door. Her eyes grew wide with surprise. She hastily glanced both ways before hurrying Mary Jane inside. Despite the deprivations of wars, Mary Jane recognized the familiar smell of turpentine and beeswax on the dust-free mahogany furniture.

Miss Bet prepared her a cup of tea made from blackberry and holly leaves and served it in a fine china cup as they sat down to exchange news. "Thank you for enduring the fetid air to come visit me," she said. She shuddered. "When I must go out, I pin a calycanthus flower to my collar and cover my nose and mouth with a handkerchief."

As they enjoyed their tea time together, Mary Jane commented that she hadn't seen the President's coachman for several days.

"You won't see him again," Miss Bet said.

Mary Jane's eyebrows arched upwards. "Do you know William Jackson? Did something happen to him?"

"Yes and no," Miss Bet said. "I didn't know him well. But until you moved into the White House, he was our only direct link for getting news from there in advance of military movements. Three days ago he ran away. My underground men found him and saw him safely to the Union lines in Fredericksburg." She took another sip of tea and set down her cup. "William had lived with the Davises almost like a member of the family. When questioned by a Union commander, he had much to tell about Confederate plans."

Mary Jane applauded. "I'm happy he ran away. The way he prayed aloud, I feared Marse would hear and suspect his loyalties." A grin slowly crept across her face. "I had no idea he and I had the same motives for being in the White House. I'm glad you were able to help him get out of Richmond."

Miss Bet pursed her lips and then continued. "Working together we're rescuing your people one by one...but there are so many of them in bondage." A shadow flitted across her face. "Each one who finds his way to freedom is a victory for us, but what are they amidst so many still held captive?"

She looked at Mary Jane and warned, "Since it was President Davis's servant and coachman who escaped, he and Varina will surely keep a closer watch on every one of you servants. You must be extremely careful to keep your identity a secret."

Mary Jane nodded. "It's easier now that I've had so much practice in guarding my lips."

A satisfied smile graced Miss Bet's face. "Since you've been gone from Church Hill, I've been taking fresh fruit, cake, books, and clothing to the prisoners in

Libby Prison as well as to our men in Ligon's. My frequent visits have made me suspect. Now more and more people of Richmond are questioning my loyalties to the Confederacy." She stuck out her jaw. "That won't stop me. Until my dying day, I will do everything I can to bring this evil enslavement to an end."

As if to prove her point, she added, "Since you've been working in the White House, my underground network has helped some prisoners to break out. They make sure the men know how to find their way to me. It's my privilege to feed them and give them shelter while we arrange for them to be taken north to freedom."

Speaking as though she'd read her mind, Miss Bet said, "Mary Jane, now you are our only channel for news from the White House. Don't risk slipping out at night again. My friend Eliza Carrington, who lives across the street from the White House, is a member of my underground. I'll arrange a meeting for you to meet Eliza soon. Until then, give Thomas any intelligence you gather."

Five days later, Mary Jane headed across the street from the White House to the Carrington house to meet Miss Bet's friend Eliza and her seamstress. Mrs. Carrington wasted no time in explaining what she wanted of the seamstress. "I need someone to pass on the information Mary Jane gathers from the White House."

"You're asking the right person." The seamstress turned to Mary Jane. "You may leave your messages for me when you bring Mrs. Davis's gowns to be mended."

She picked up a garment and showed her how to hide information inside the waistband. "Tuck your note inside and stitch it together before bringing the gown to be mended. "If you've no time to do that, just stitch the information into a fold of the skirt before you drop it off," she said.

"I can do that," Mary Jane said.

"Mary Jane, I'll visit Eliza after your appointed day to bring Varina's gowns," Miss Bet said. "If you can't get a message to me, watch for Thomas."

Miss Bet reached into her pocket and pulled out a strange-looking pendant. It was a peach pit with a tiny carved three-leafed clover, dangling inside it. Handing it to Mary Jane she added, "Now that you are the only member of our underground who is actively spying on Jefferson Davis, you need to wear this to identify yourself as one of us.

Mary Jane turned the necklace over in her hand, trying hard to keep her curiosity under control.

"You must keep it hidden under your collar," Miss Bet cautioned. "If ever I send a member of our network to you to receive information, his clover will be hanging from his watch chain. When the clover is upside down, it's safe to exchange information with him. Gently pat your neck to let him know you've seen it. But if the clover is right side up, keep your lips sealed."

Mary Jane nodded, but felt a bit uneasy. *May I never have to rely on a peach pit for safety.*

Chapter Fourteen

By mid-August Mary Jane's daily duties as a household servant in the Confederate White House included assisting in meal preparation, looking after the children, and helping keep the mansion dust free. On the second Tuesday of each month, she crossed the street with Mistress Davis's torn gowns.

Varina Davis frequently left the White House to attend sewing parties. She and the women of Richmond stitched uniforms, undergarments, shirts, and blankets for the troops, while others knitted socks or prepared bandages.

Mary Jane never knew when General Lee would arrive with his commanding officers, so she made sure that the President's office and his private reception room were always spotless. After polishing the furniture, she lingered over his desk, now piled high with maps of fortifications and statistics about his troops. She sifted through his recent correspondence using her photographic memory to "copy" each letter to imprint its contents on her mind. Then, she placed it back exactly where it had been.

One Monday afternoon, the pile of correspondence was larger than usual. She dropped her duster and scanned each letter. One of them outlined detailed plans for another battle at Manassas. A second one confirmed that John Pope was in command of the newly formed Union Army of Virginia. "McClellan is on his way to join Pope, heading toward Manassas," the letter warned. "If he succeeds, our troops will be greatly outnumbered."

An updated memo from General Lee detailed his plans to strike Pope's army. "Jackson and Longstreet will cut him off before that happens."

After the evening meal, Mary Jane tucked the children in for the night. She needed to write down what she had read. She glanced at the calendar. Learning about the plans, couldn't have happened at a better time. *I can pass this information on tomorrow when I take Mrs. Davis's gowns to be mended."*

That evening she reviewed everything she knew about the Rebel plans. Carefully, she recorded each detail as she had read it. When she finished, she folded the note as tightly as she could and hid it temporarily in her shoe. In the morning, she would pick up Mrs. Davis's gowns and pin the paper inside the folds of one of the skirts.

Mid-morning the next day, she carried the gowns across the street to Eliza Carrington's home. *Thank you, Jesus, I don't have to deliver this message tonight.* The seamstress had arrived before her and stood in the wide front hall next to the credenza. They greeted each other and shared pleasantries. *Why doesn't she tell me her name? In Miss Bet's home white folks always addressed themselves by giving their names.* Then she remembered Miss Bet's caution. *"Mary Jane, the walls have ears. You must remember to weigh every word carefully before it leaves your mouth."*

She pointed toward the skirt, nodded and handed it to Mrs. Carrington's guest. The nameless seamstress accepted it with a quick raising and lowering or her chin. Mary Jane left without a word and hastened back across the street to the White House.

Back in her servant's quarters, she drew in a long breath, blew it out slowly, and sat down to contemplate her life since she'd come to work for Mrs. Davis. *Today I have fulfilled my role as a spy without having to sneak out at dusk—and without detection.* She relived her accomplishments in reverse order. Thus far she'd passed on strategic battle plans to Miss Bet with no slip-ups in keeping her identity a secret. She was helping Miss Bet in her fight to end slavery.

However, as those thoughts led her back to Church Hill, her eyes clouded. She missed Wilson. She longed to see him. To feel his loving, protective arms holding her close. *If only this war would end so that I could go home to be with him forever.*

By fall Mary Jane and everybody else in Richmond longed for peace: for those comfortable days before the embargo and before Northern armies stopped train deliveries by tearing up tracks and ties, tipping over locomotives, and cars and blowing up bridges; and one could buy food and necessities. They prayed for days when all the wounded would heal, and prisons would not resound with the cries of injured men. They grieved for fresh air and the fragrance of blooming magnolias, instead of the foul odor of rotting wounds and unburied corpses.

One mid-September morning when she happened by the newspaper office, Mary Jane lingered to read the bulletin board.

> CONFEDERATE TROOPS UNDER
> LEE LOSE TO UNION FORCES
> AT ANTIETAM, MARYLAND.
> 1550 KILLED
> 7750 WOUNDED
> 1000 MISSING
> NORTHERN LOSSES WERE
> MUCH HIGHER

About a week later when she went into President Davis's office to dust it, the *Dispatch was* lying open on top of his desk. Mary Jane hastened to scan its pages. A summary of the September 17 battle at Antietam stated that McClellan and his Union forces had stopped Lee and the Confederate troops. In this bloody battle 26,000 men were killed, wounded or missing, and Lee had withdrawn to Virginia. Another article stated that the Union troops suffered more than half the casualties. Her heart sank at the tremendous cost to both sides. Would this war never end?

On September 22, President Lincoln issued his preliminary Emancipation Proclamation. The Confederates had until January 1, 1863, to end the fighting and rejoin the Union. If they failed to do so, all slaves in the rebellious states would be free.

H'm? Our goal is to end slavery everywhere. Not just in the Confederate states. It sounds like President Lincoln's Emancipation Proclamation is limited. Her brow wrinkled as she thought about it. *Can President Lincoln force the Confederate states to free their slaves? Or will those states simply ignore the proclamation?* She'd have to wait and see.

Mary Jane found out just what President Lincoln meant on January 1, 1863, when he issued the final Proclamation which *freed all slaves held by the Confederate States.* Living in the Confederate White House, she had to contain her joy, though she applauded in her heart. But she and the other house servants walked about with lightness in their steps and exchanged happy smiles. *If only I could be with Wilson right now. He would pull out his fiddle. Then, we would dance and sing to celebrate this announcement with thanksgiving.*

Having served Mistress Davis for a year and a half, Mary Jane felt confident in her role as a spy. Whenever visiting generals showed up to inform President Davis of their strategies, she served them with ease, lingering within earshot of their conversation around the dining table, hoping to hear more.

Instead of performing her duties with a churning

stomach, she nursed a lonesome heart. She thought of Wilson every day, and more so each night. She missed talking with him at mealtimes. She missed holding hands as they took Jake for a walk. And most of all, she missed snuggling in his strong, comforting arms. *I hope he's well. I wonder if he's delivering the information I've gathered for Miss Bet.*

One morning after she finished her breakfast chores, Mistress Davis came into the kitchen somewhat disturbed. "Today we have several new generals coming for the noon meal. What a day to be shorthanded. Bessie is ill, and I need to take her place with the preparations." She handed Mary Jane a basket of turnips, carrots, and onions. "Please wash these vegetables and chop them into bite-size pieces. When you are finished, set the table for our guests." Then she sat down at the kitchen table and turned the pages of her cookbook until she'd found what she wanted. She spoke as though talking to herself, "I do hope the men will find the claret soup to their liking. And the chocolate jelly cake that Bessie made yesterday."

Mary Jane prepared the vegetables and headed to the dining room. After spreading the snowy white tablecloth, she counted out the number of plates needed, set them in place and went to the drawer to get the fine silver. To her surprise, it had been replaced with the everyday tableware used only for family dining.

She paused momentarily, pondering this change. *Mistress Davis enjoyed serving her guests in the finest way possible. What happened to her silver?* Then she remembered. The South was short of metals to meet the wartime needs. Citizens were urged to donate their church bells so the iron could be made into cannons and their fine silver to be melted down to meet other needs. St. John's bell was still calling people to worship. She wondered for how long. The Davises must have given up their sterling silver flatware.

Shortly before one o'clock, President Davis welcomed General Lee and four men that Mary Jane did not recognize. She memorized their names as he greeted them: *General Longstreet. General Hooker. General Ewell. General Hill.*

War talk began immediately. *Gettysburg.* She knew that was somewhere in neighboring Pennsylvania. "My troops will move from Fredericksburg into the Shenandoah Valley," Lee said. He addressed the man on his right. "Longstreet," he said, "Hooker and his cavalry forces will support you." He nodded toward the other two men. "Ewell, I want you to position your men across the Susquehanna River. Hill, you need to be at the ready behind the mountains in Chambersburg."

The meal ended, the generals departed, and Mary

Jane reviewed what she learned as she cleared the dining room table. *This information must be delivered to Miss Bet tonight. But she won't be expecting to see me.*

Since Miss Bet avoided suspicion by no longer venturing in sight of the White House, she'd have to search for her. That meant she must work fast to record all the battle details, find her, deliver the message, and scoot home before curfew. She glanced at the mantel clock. Since it was early summer, sundown didn't occur until after eight o'clock. *I can do it.*

Mary Jane washed the dishes, wiped off the table, and made sure everything had been put away in its proper place. Then she slipped off to her quarters to prepare her notes. She reached into the drawer where she kept the paper that Thomas supplied her. *Oh, no. I used the last piece two days ago.*

She looked at the clock and charged back to the White House to the President's office. Checking to make sure Mrs. Davis was not around, she darted inside and headed for the drawer where President Davis stored his paper. Just as she pulled the drawer open, she heard the echo of footsteps, approaching in the hallway. She recognized that sound. It was Mrs. Davis, and she was headed right by the open door.

Mary Jane had no reason to be in the President's office at this hour, and she could see no place to hide.

She dropped to the floor, easing the drawer shut with her hip.

Mrs. Davis stopped in the doorway, arms akimbo. "Mary Jane, what are you doing here?" Mary Jane's breath caught in her throat.

Caught.

Chapter Fifteen

With her entire body on high alert, Mary Jane forced herself to play the part of a simple-minded black. She directed her gaze to the floor in keeping with her role as a humble servant and prayed that Mistress Davis couldn't hear her heart thudding against her breastbone. "Billy has lost a shoe again, Mistress Davis. He had been playing in Marse's office this morning. I came in to look for it."

"Well, see that you find it and take it back to him." She turned to go and then stopped abruptly. "Before you leave today, straighten up his room and put things in their proper places, including his shoes." With that final assignment, she disappeared down the hallway.

Mary Jane snatched some paper and headed back to her room. She thought about hanging the red shirt on the line but changed her mind. This late in the day, Miss Bet wouldn't be expecting it and might not notice. Back in her quarters, she recorded the generals' names and their battle plans. She folded her note tightly and slid it into the heel of her shoe. She was about to slip out when she remembered she had to straighten Billy's room. She scurried back to the White House, flew into his room and gathered his clothing off the floor faster than ever.

As she left her quarters, the summer sun was moving slowly westward. Deepening shadows in the dooryard set her pulse racing. She had never left her quarters this late. *What if Miss Bet concludes I'm not coming and goes home?* She glanced at the sun again. *If I can't find her, I'll have to take the message up to Church Hill myself. How can I do that and get back to my quarters before curfew?*

She closed her eyes and took a deep breath to steady her nerves, and then gagged on the noxious smell that hung like a pall over the city. She had forgotten her scarf. *If I'm caught, I will become a nameless prisoner. I may be whipped or worse.* She cupped her nose in her hands, inhaled several times and straightened her shoulders.

Regardless of what may happen to me, I must deliver this message tonight.

There was no escape from the presence of death, nor from the moans and feeble cries of mangled men in the streets. She wended her way through back streets to avoid others who might be about and made her way through a maze of over-crowded hospital tents. Her feet kept pace with her heartbeats pounding in her head. Suddenly, she caught a glimpse of Miss Bet ahead of her, not too far from the intersection. She quickened her steps.

Miss Bet must have heard her running. She turned, paused and then moved on ever so slowly into the shadows until they were side by side.

Wordlessly, Mary Jane bent down, retrieved the priceless message from her shoe and gave it to her. Miss Bet hugged her close. "Thank you, Mary Jane. You are a brave woman." She looked into her eyes and whispered, "Now, go quickly."

Mary Jane turned back toward the White House amidst the darkening shadows. Keeping to the darker side of the street, she sprinted along until she was nearly breathless. Before she had gone more than one more block, the hair on the back of her neck stood up. She sensed someone following close behind her. *Could it be another servant trying to make it home before curfew?*

Or might it be the authorities looking for someone to arrest?

Just ahead was a broad intersection. She would have to leave the safety of the shadows. She pressed her elbows against her waist to make her body as small as possible. Fear of being out so late at night fueled her efforts. As she fled across the intersection, she risked a quick backward look. No one in sight. *Is my imagination playing tricks on me?* She bolted through the next block.

She was only a block from the White House when again she heard footsteps. This time there was no mistaking them. *Someone is following me.* Her pulse quickened. She ran faster. So did whoever was behind her. She slowed down. So did her pursuer. She dared not take time to glance back.

She could see the Davis mansion just ahead. She streaked past the last familiar buildings, charged into her quarters, and slammed the door.

Once inside she leaned against it, panting, and peered out her small window. A figure paused in front of her quarters and then melted into the shadows. *Who was that? What did he want? Why did he follow me all the way home? Why had he let me go?*

She lay awake for hours as questions swirled through her mind.

The next morning as she went about her breakfast

duties, she still felt uneasy. She couldn't get last night's fright out of her mind. Whoever had followed her knew where she lived. Would he report her to the Davises? She hoped she'd never have to slip out again.

When the baker arrived with his morning delivery, she hurried to meet him at the gate. "Good morning, Thomas."

"Mornin', Mary Jane," he replied, as he stuck his thumb into the pocket of his trousers. He glanced down, and Mary Jane's gaze followed his to the clover on his belt.

His clover dangled upside down. She could speak freely. She hastened to tell him what happened the previous night.

"Calm down, Mary Jane. I know you are upset, but don't worry."

Mary Jane's eyes widened. "Not worry. What if I were caught. I-I-I could be…"

Thomas held up his hand to stop her from continuing that train of thought. Before she could say anything more, he added, "It's not what you think." He spoke calmly. "On my way home last night I saw you with Miss Bet. I followed you in case you were caught out after curfew."

A heavy load of worry slid from Mary Jane's shoulders. At the same time, she recalled Miss Bet's comment the day she agreed to join the spy ring.

Mary Jane's fears slowly dissolved. She lowered her eyes, ashamed that she had acted so fearfully. "Thank you, Thomas," she said as she took the shortbread and hot cross buns and returned to the White House kitchen.

By the summer of 1863, Mary Jane knew that her spying in the White House was paying off for the Union. The tide had turned against the South after the Union soldiers defeated the Confederates at Gettysburg on July 1-3 in the bloodiest battle of the war. The Southern army had been short of men, supplies, and food. Now the starving survivors were carried home to Richmond in tatters along with the wounded, the dead, and their Northern prisoners.

The individual funeral processions for officers with riderless horses and boots reversed in the stirrups, followed by bands playing mournful dirges were rare by now, though these men were still buried in individual graves. But there were so many deaths that gravediggers still could not keep up. Bodies of enlisted soldiers were taken straight to burial grounds and interred in mass graves. When their names were known, they were scrawled on wooden shingles stuck upright in the ground above them.

One day when Mary Jane was on an errand, she

chanced another visit up Church Hill to see Miss Bet. How she wished she was going to see Wilson, but it was too risky to write to him. Since all able men had been drafted, along the way, she saw only weary women in the streets. Many of them tilled the fields and tended the gardens alone. Their children followed behind them in tow, since there was no one left at home to care for them. Mary Jane stepped to the curbside and lowered her gaze as the law demanded. *It's a good thing they can't see the fire in my eyes.*

As before, Miss Bet opened the door only a crack and pulled her inside. "Are you sure you weren't followed?" she asked.

"Yes," Mary Jane answered. "I'm sure. "

"Well then, I'm glad to see you came. Come into the parlor. We can chat while I work in private."

"How is Wilson, Miss Bet?" She swallowed trying to keep her tears inside. "Is he all right?"

Miss Bet drew her close. "Yes, Mary Jane. Wilson is well. He misses you. He's doing what he can to bring this dreadful war to an end, just as you are." She paused until Mary Jane relaxed in her embrace. "Wilson delivers the information you bring to me." She looked into Mary Jane's face. "Someday, you two can tell your grandchildren how you worked together to end this conflict."

"I wish I could see him again," Mary whispered wistfully.

Miss Bet patted Mary Jane's hand. "One of these days you will."

Mary Jane wiped her eyes and swallowed. Her beloved husband was in as much danger as she was. Maybe more. Some soldiers might go easy on a woman caught spying. But a male spy? They would hang him as soon as look at him. Mary Jane shook her head and shuddered. Then, looking at Miss Bet, she asked, "What can I do to help you?"

Miss Bet handed her a pair of scissors. "I'm delighted to have your company *and* grateful for your help." She nodded toward a stack of linens on the table.

"What are you doing with these linens?"

"First we must cut them into four or five-inch squares."

"And then what?"

"That's when the real work," Miss Bet said. "We pull some of the threads on the squares and then scrape them into lint." She nodded toward some sharp knives on the kitchen table. "Doctors pack the lint into open wounds to help control bleeding." She grimaced. "With so many wounded, there is never enough lint." She picked up a knife and showed Mary Jane how to hold the cloth taut with one hand and scrape it with the other.

Mary Jane learned quickly, and as they worked, Miss Bet caught her up on the activities of her brother John. "John was given repeated medical exemptions when the draft began. Little by little, he became involved in my underground work, until he became very helpful as a courier to the North. But then Southern manpower dwindled, and he was drafted to serve in the army."

"Oh, no." Mary Jane's stomach churned at the news.

Miss Bet sighed and drew in a deep breath. "He was able to stay out of the battle for a brief time. However, in May he was forced to the front lines at Cold Harbor."

"That's dreadful." Mary Jane slid to the edge of her seat to give her full attention to Miss Bet. "Then what happened?"

"He refused to fight against the Northern troops. So, he deserted and escaped to Philadelphia to live with our sister Anna."

Mary Jane gasped when Miss Bet mentioned desertion. "Wearing that Confederate uniform must have been agonizing to him."

Miss Bet nodded, and the conversation switched to small talk about Mary Jane's life in the White House. Mary Jane finished picking the last square, laid down her knife, and stretched her fingers. "You're right, Miss Bet," she said with a chuckle. "That was real work."

"Yes, Mary Jane. But it's the primary activity for

ladies' relief societies. By preparing my share of lint, I'm acting as a loyal citizen of Richmond. But secretly I do it in support of our wounded Northern prisoners."

Miss Bet sat back and stretched. "I'm still permitted to take food and books to the prison, but now, the guards examine them. They refuse to let the men talk with me." A shadow darkened her face. "They stand close by to make sure they don't."

She planted her hands on her hips and added, "I've devised a different system for gathering news." She picked up a book from her library and showed Mary Jane where she had made a very thin split in the spine. "I hid a message in there."

"That was a great idea, Miss Bet."

Miss Bet agreed. She pursed her lips. "It worked for several visits. But if the guards had taken a closer look at the books, they might have detected the slits. So I came up with another method. And that's where I could use some help."

She picked up another book, opened it, and pointed to tiny pinholes barely detectable beneath certain letters, words, and numbers. "The prisoners spell out the messages to me one letter at a time. If I hold these pages in front of a candle, I can see the holes clearly and read the message. This idea works, but it's as time-consuming as scraping lint."

She laid the marked book on the table. "After I pick up my books from the prisoners, I transcribe the information from the pinprick messages the men have made. Then I hide them under the driver's seat on the farm wagon at the stables." She paused and looked directly into Mary Jane's eyes. "When the wagon arrives at the farm, Wilson checks for messages. If he finds one, he delivers it to Harrison's Landing that same evening."

At the mention of her husband, a lump grew in Mary Jane's throat.

Miss Bet drew her close. "You and Wilson are true warriors for our cause, and the North depends on you. There is no one else in Virginia who is capable of doing what you two do."

Mary Jane wiped her eyes. "I know that. It makes our separation more bearable." She glanced at the clock on the mantle. "I'm must get back to the White House. If I stay away too long, Mistress Davis will notice."

Miss Bet reached for her hand and gave it a squeeze. "Come up when you can, and don't fret when you can't. Now, be careful returning home,'" she whispered.

"I will," said Mary Jane as she slipped out the back entrance.

Chapter Sixteen

A few days after helping Miss Bet pick lint, Mary Jane met Thomas at the White House gate. "Good morning." he bellowed with his usual enthusiasm. Fall had arrived in Richmond, and everyone appreciated the cooler weather. As Mary Jane reached out to take the sweet-smelling loaves of fresh bread, he slipped a note into her hands. Their eyes met. He brushed his index finger over his lips and then headed off for his next delivery.

Mary Jane tucked the note into her apron pocket without reading it. As soon as she was alone, she slipped into the parlor and pulled out the note. She immediately recognized Miss Bet's handwriting.

The message was short:

> *URGENT. COME UP TO CHURCH*
> *HILL THIS MORNING.*

Mary Jane's knees buckled. Something must have happened to Wilson. Or Miss Bet. Otherwise, she wouldn't risk sending for her in broad daylight. Feeling faint, she sank onto a chair, her knees suddenly weak, and her mind a swirl of what-ifs.

It was Tuesday, the day Mistress Davis usually left the children in her care while she went off to help her friends sew for the troops. *I can't take them with me, and I don't dare leave them with another servant. Mistress Davis wouldn't approve.* As she returned to the kitchen to finish breakfast preparations, she heard Mistress Davis's footsteps.

"Mary Jane," she said, stopping in the doorway. "The President is away today. I'm taking the children with me to visit a friend outside Richmond. We'll be leaving mid-morning and be gone for the day."

Mary Jane's worries lightened as she scurried to get breakfast on the table. As soon as Mistress Davis and the children finished their meal, Mary Jane washed the dishes and swept the kitchen floor. Then, she grabbed the feather duster and headed to the parlor. When she finished there, she charged into the dining room and attacked the legs of the table and polished the sideboard with a fury.

About an hour later, Mistress Davis was ready to depart. "We won't be back 'til late afternoon," she said as Mary Jane helped her herd the children out the door and into the carriage.

Mary Jane glanced up as the parlor clock struck ten. *Urgent. Come up to Church Hill this morning.* If she left immediately, she'd have plenty of time to get back before Mistress Davis returned with the children.

She dashed out the kitchen door to her servant's quarters, grabbed the sack she carried on errands, and headed out. Normally it was a fifteen-minute walk up Church Hill, but these days it would take longer because of the new makeshift hospital tents set up, blocking many streets.

Had she not been so worried about Miss Bet, Mary Jane would have enjoyed the lone bright spot left in the city: neglected flower gardens still bloomed as if in defiance of all the horror. The cryptic message, branded on her mind, propelled Mary Jane along as fast as she dared walk without attracting attention.

By the time she arrived at Miss Bet's mansion, her thumping heart was battering her breastbone. She crept around to the rear of the mansion and knocked on the familiar door.

As the door swung wide, she felt as if her heart leapt from her rib cage. "Wilson!" Her legs turned rubbery as familiar arms caught her, drew her into his arms and held her in a vice grip. "My precious Mary Jane," Wilson whispered as they stood locked in each other's arms.

"I missed you so much," she cried. "These past two years without you have been so hard. And trying to keep my feelings inside…" Her sobs increased.

By and by, Wilson loosened his grip on her. He cradled her face in his hands and looked deeply into her eyes before their lips melted together.

Meanwhile, Miss Bet stood misty-eyed in the doorway, waiting.

When Wilson released her, Mary Jane turned toward Miss Bet. "I can't find adequate words to thank you." She enfolded the woman in a grateful embrace as another flood of grateful tears cascaded down her face.

Miss Bet kissed Mary Jane's forehead and released her. She smiled at Wilson and said, "Now it's time for tea." She had prepared dainty tea biscuits, gingerbread nuts, and snow pudding for them. It was a bountiful feast, despite all the food shortages in the city. "Please sit down," she said as she joined them around the table.

After a bit of light chatter, Miss Bet rose. Looking at Mary Jane and then Wilson, she said. "I'm so sorry that you can't spend the entire day together."

"Both Mistress Davis and Marse are away today. I can stay until two and still get home before they return."

"That's wonderful," Miss Bet said. "I'll leave you until then."

The pastries looked inviting. But their longing to hold each other overpowered their interest in anything else. Wilson drew Mary Jane close to his heart, and she nestled against the warmth of his muscular arms. "I missed ya ever'day," Wilson said. He paused. "I dint think ya'd be away fer so long."

Mary Jane nodded. When she found her voice, she said, "With each message I passed on to Miss Bet, I asked the Lord to protect you if you might be the one to deliver it down river."

"I was sure you'd do that." He swallowed. "As I rowed back ta the farm after each delivery, I ast the Lord ta keep ya safe. And to bring ya home soon." He looked at her and added, "And here ya are." And then he whispered, "How I wish ya could stay."

"If only this dreadful war would end. Then I could come home for good…" She was unable to finish. That time seemed impossibly far away.

Wilson drew her close. "Let's not talk about the war. I jist want ta hold ya."

All too soon, the mantle clock chimed. Two chimes. Mary Jane blinked to hold her tears. "One day we'll be together for keeps."

"Hold tight to that thought, Mary Jane," Wilson whispered into her hair, "and I will, too."

Miss Bet rejoined them. She drew Mary Jane close and kissed her cheek. "Goodbye, my child," she whispered.

Mary Jane thanked her. "Thank you for this precious gift, Miss Bet."

Wilson took Mary Jane's hand and led her to the side door and down the porch steps. They shared one more tearful embrace before Mary Jane turned and forced her feet to take her down the hill. Memories of that priceless morning would sustain her for whatever lay ahead.

Mid-morning one early November day, just as Mary Jane finished scrubbing the cream-colored carpet in the President's private reception room, Marse Davis strode in with General Lee and several other grim-faced men in gray uniforms. Lee glanced down at the carpet, and then at his boots, as though he feared he would muddy it. Then, apparently deciding it didn't matter, he cleared his throat and unrolled a map on the mahogany table. The others gathered around him.

When the general mentioned locations with unfamiliar names, Mary Jane bustled about the room, straining to hear what he was saying.

"Rappahannock River. Kelly's Ford. Brandy Station. Rappahannock Station. Culpeper."

Mary Jane repeated the words in her mind as she slowly worked her way closer with her feather duster. Once near the table, she concentrated on the determined voices as they worked out their attack strategy.

General Lee focused his attention on Rappahannock Station. "Our one connection to the northern side of the river is a single pontoon bridge right here," he said. "A bridgehead on the north bank is our only protection. We *must* hold that bridgehead."

The one called General Early added, "By doing that, we can threaten any flank movement the enemy might make above or below the bridge."

Lee nodded. "That would compel Meade to divide his forces." He drew in a deep breath. "We must guard our plans carefully. They must not fall into enemy hands." He rolled up the map and looked each general in the eye as if to challenge him. "We'll soon teach those Northern boys a thing or two."

When Mary Jane heard General Lee's threat, she dropped her feather duster. Massa Davis looked her way and scowled. She scooped it up and continued her work. This time, she was glad to be "unworthy of further attention." *I must get word to Miss Bet.* To renew her courage, she flattened her palm against the clover under her collar. *I will not be afraid.* She squared her shoulders. *I will be brave.*

As soon as the door closed behind the men, she flew to the desk, unrolled the map, and searched for the Rappahannock River. *Aha. There it is.* One by one she traced with her finger the places the men had discussed. As she re-rolled the map, heavy footsteps sounded outside the door. She snatched up her duster and darted to the opposite side of the room. The door opened, and General Early stepped inside.

Mary Jane busied herself in the far corner of the room, hoping he'd ignore her. She held her breath as he walked over to the side of the table where he had stood looking at the map. He paused, looked around, and then stooped down and picked up his hat. He left as quickly as he had entered.

Mary Jane collapsed into a chair. "Miss Bet told me not to risk delivering any more messages at dusk. But time is short. I must tell her tonight what these plans are," she whispered under her breath.

Today was Mistress Davis's afternoon to gather with other Confederate women to sew shirts and knit socks for the troops. She instructed Mary Jane to care for the children and left the White House as soon as the men took their leave.

Throughout the afternoon the children kept Mary

Jane busy, stopping their squabbles, looking for lost toys, and picking up after they left things in childish disarray.

Two-year-old Billy followed her around, getting underfoot and slowing her down in her routine duties. It was her evening to wash the dishes and tidy up the kitchen, and she struggled to keep him occupied long enough to complete her work. Just as she finished, he began to cry. She gathered him into her arms and held him until his tears stopped. She took him to the kitchen and gave him a spoonful of warm lard and syrup. Eventually, he fell asleep in her arms, and she carried him to his bed.

She had not had one minute alone to write down the attack plans. Throughout the afternoon she had mentally repeated the locations to keep from forgetting any important details. She glanced at the clock and grimaced. It was too late to slip away this evening.

She returned to her quarters, rested a few minutes, and then set to work recording in detail what she had heard. As usual, she folded her notes into a tiny square and slipped it into the heel of her shoe. She would pass it on to Thomas come morning.

Chapter Seventeen

The next morning as Mary Jane prepared breakfast, she hummed under her breath to hide her frustration at not being able to deliver her message to Miss Bet the previous evening. As she worked, she watched for Thomas through the kitchen window. When he approached with his usual delivery of soda bread and hot cross buns, she slipped out to meet him at the gate.

"Good morning, Thomas."

"Good morning to you, Mary Jane." He thrust his right thumb into his pocket with a bold movement. His cloverleaf was dangling upright. When Mary Jane saw it, her jaw dropped to her chest. It was not safe to talk. She looked into Thomas's eyes and nodded. *The information I have* must *be delivered tonight, and I'm the only one who can do that.*

A few years ago, after she'd returned from Philadelphia, she and Wilson had wandered about the streets of Richmond looking for runaways. She knew her way around the city. But now many of the streets were blocked, making it impossible to travel directly to a specific destination. *Even if Miss Bet were expecting me, it would be hard for her to find me tonight.*

She struggled to keep calm as she carried the pastries inside, but a slow churning began in her stomach. Images of what might happen if anyone caught her out after dark jockeyed for places in her mind and set her heartbeats to thrashing in her ears. She set the baked goods down on the heavy oak table and clawed her cheeks dragging her fingers downward as fear and duty wrestled inside her. She thought of Wilson. *My brave husband risks his life to deliver Miss Bet's messages to Harrison's Landing. But I don't know if I have enough courage to risk mine tonight. It's November, and it's dark by 4:30.*

She thought of Miss Bet. *She's trusted me to work with her network. She has done so much for Wilson and me. I will not fail her now.* And then she considered what might happen if she didn't deliver this message in time for the Northern troops to prepare for an attack. *I will do it. For Wilson. For Miss Bet. And for myself and all of my people.*

To cement her determination, Mary Jane sucked in a long breath and prayed. *Lord, I'm afraid. Please help me find Miss Bet. And please get me safely home.*

She was finishing up her breakfast duties when Mistress Davis appeared in the doorway. "Today I want you to wash the windows in the kitchen and the dining room. After you've cleaned them, sweep and scrub the front porch steps."

Mary Jane eyed the tall windows, stifled the giant sigh building up inside her, and went to fetch the ladder. Added to her usual duties, that would keep her occupied for most of the day.

It was dark by the time she finished her work and returned to her quarters. She checked to make sure the battle plans were still inside her heel and peered out the door. Nobody was in sight. Good. After her last frightening delivery, she had never wanted to make another one. She prayed again for the Lord's help and protection before sneaking out into the darkness.

She yanked the door shut behind her. *Thunk.* The inside latch dropped into place. Her heart sank. *Well, Mary Jane, you can't worry about that now.* She tightened her scarf over her nose and mouth. *I must get this message to Miss Bet tonight.*

She dared not think about the consequences of a failed mission. She shoved that dread to the back of her mind and set off down the street. A soon-to-be-full moon was the only light she had to guide her steps. The summer heat was gone, but the nauseating stench remained.

As she meandered her way across an intersection and into the third block, someone slipped out of the shadows and touched her arm.

Mary Jane gasped. "Miss Bet." A sigh of relief along with a prayer of thanksgiving escaped her lips. She retrieved the notes from her shoe and handed them to Miss Bet. "Big battle plans," she whispered. "I'm sorry I couldn't get them to you sooner."

"No need to explain," Miss Bet said, tucking the notes under her bonnet. "You're helping to win this war in a way no one else can." She squeezed Mary Jane's hand. "Now be extra careful going back to your quarters."

As Mary Jane turned toward home, an explosion rent the air. Flames shot upward. Billowing clouds of acrid smoke spread quickly. Crowds of panicked people appeared through the smoke. Mary Jane froze in place, her mind reeling. *Was this Union sabotage or was it an accident? Should I tell Miss Bet I've locked myself out and then head for the nearest hidey-hole? I would be safe there for tonight. But what would I do in the morning?*

While she was trying to get her bearings and decide what to do, Miss Bet disappeared. Smoke obscured the faint light from the pale moon. She'd have to find her way back to the White House by an unfamiliar route. *Help, Lord.* In desperation, she chose a street that she sensed ran parallel to the one she usually traveled.

She had not gone far when shouting men and galloping horses pulling fire-fighting equipment poured out to fight the fire. One fireman bumped her as he dragged a water hose. Mary Jane stumbled but kept running. She had covered one short block when another explosion occurred. Startled, she tripped and twisted her ankle.

Ash from the fire floated down around her like dirty snowflakes. Scrambling to her feet, she peered through the thick smoke and limped along as fast as the pain in her ankle allowed. And then she remembered the latch on the door back in her quarters. *How will I get inside when I get back?* She tried to hold her fears at bay. *Maybe I was wrong. Maybe the latch didn't drop when I yanked the door shut. Maybe I just thought it did.* She voiced another silent prayer.

Mary Jane picked her way through the debris, keeping in the shadows until she finally reached her quarters. She shoved against the door. It didn't budge. "Oooch." She fell to the ground, and her twisted ankle pained her all the more. After scrambling to her feet, she ignored the sharp pain and tried again to force the door open. It was secured in place. She must get it to open before someone discovered her outside after curfew. *Or pay the ultimate price.*

Flattening her palms against the door, she pushed with all the strength she had left. The latch inside rattled. The sound reverberated in the silent night. She dared not try it again, lest someone hear it. The door did not budge.

Mary Jane drew in some deep breaths and tried to think clearly. Every minute outside made it more likely that someone would discover her. She glanced fearfully around; her ear acutely attuned to every sound; her eyes watchful for the slightest movement.

Then, as the haze drifted away from the moon, she thought of something that might work. If she could get her arm through that small window to the right of the door, she might be able to reach the fallen bar. She squatted on the step and pulled off a shoe. Mustering all the strength she could, she slammed the heel against the corner of the window. The glass cracked. Another blow and she had knocked a hole in it. A large shard broke loose and fell inside. She struck the window with another blow and listened for footsteps that indicated someone had heard the shattering glass and was coming to investigate. *Silence. Beautiful.* She felt the edge slowly to be sure she had knocked all the glass out. She did not want to try to explain a nasty cut to Mistress Davis or any of the servants.

She yanked up the bottom of her skirt and wrapped it around her hand and forearm. Ignoring the throbbing pain from her twisted ankle, she flattened her body against the door and very slowly slipped her arm inside. Her fingers walked the wall until they reached the door frame. Pulling her shoulder closer, she stretched out her arm until it ached. Her fingers searched for the latch and found it.

Thank goodness it was my ankle and not my wrist that I've sprained. Little by little Mary Jane nudged the bar until one stronger poke dislodged it. *Thank you, Lord.*

She dragged herself inside and collapsed on her bed amidst tears of rejoicing and relief. Another successful mission completed.

When she awakened the next morning, she thought about the previous night's frightful experiences. She had done her part to warn the Union troops of the Confederate plans. She thought of Wilson. *Maybe he's the courier who'll carry Miss Bet's message on to Harrison's Landing.*

She was eager to learn the outcome of the battle. For the next several days she passed by the office of the *Dispatch* to read the bulletin board. The news she'd been waiting for was posted two days later. It was detailed, and it took her several trips by the office to read it all without arousing suspicion.

As Mary Jane made her way back to the White House, she mulled over in her mind what she'd read. According to the bulletin, the battle for control of the bridgehead began on November 7 and General Lee's most experienced troops, the Louisiana Tigers, were charged with guarding it. But the general had miscalculated what the Union's forces were planning. In a fierce nighttime attack, the Union army captured the bridgehead and took more than 1600 prisoners. General Lee was forced to retreat to south of the Rapidan River until spring while the Northern army occupied the vicinity of Brandy Station and Culpeper County.

Mary Jane rejoiced in her heart that the North was gradually gaining ground in the struggle to win this war. *My message got through on time.*

Chapter Eighteen

Northerners call it the "War of the Rebellion," and Southerners call it the "War of Northern Aggression." Whatever the name, the devastating War Between the States, after dragging on for three years, had finally turned in favor of the Union forces. Mary Jane and everybody else in Richmond longed for the days of peace when food was plentiful, along with other necessities, and some niceties as well.

They pined for an end to the fighting that had resulted in thousands of wounded and dying men being brought to their city that was already bloated from casualties of previous battles. For the return of husbands and fathers and brothers. For the burial of the accumulated deceased from earlier battles. And for the return of fresh air.

Mary Jane had been sorely pained by the carnage at Cold Harbor the previous July when in a mere twenty minutes, the Union forces under General Ulysses S. Grant suffered 7,000 casualties. And then his soldiers missed an opportunity to cut off the Confederate rail lines which would have enabled them to capture Petersburg. She couldn't help but wonder if she had missed learning of that plan, if she had failed her people.

One December evening as she passed President Davis's study, after putting the children to bed, Mistress Davis brushed by her and rushed inside. Mary Jane glanced through the open door. The bedeviled President sat at his desk holding his head in his hands. "Another of our servants has disappeared," Mistress Davis bemoaned. "Foolish boy. I suppose he's run away to join the Northern troops."

Mary Jane hadn't seen several of the household servants for a week or so and assumed that they had been dismissed. Now she crept close to hear what was said.

President Davis's brow knitted, and his shoulders sagged. "More and more of our servants are being deluded and deserting us," he said. "I don't trust any of them not to run off, taking some of our possessions with them." He pounded the desk with his fists. "Nor to refuse a bribe to sabotage us in some devilish way."

Mistress Davis sighed and collapsed into a chair beside her husband. "They're so easily lured away." She frowned. "And so simple-minded. They think they'll be better off in the North on their own."

"One of them is not simple-minded." President Davis bellowed.

Mistress Davis stared at him as though he'd cursed God. "Why do you say that?"

President Davis leaped to his feet and slammed his desk with both hands. "Unless our walls have ears, somebody in this place is leaking information to the Northern forces." A fierce scowl distorted his face. "I wondered how it was possible for those blue bellies to be waiting for us at Rappahannock River. And since then it seems more than once that the Union anticipated the plans discussed right here in the White House."

Varina Davis grimaced. "Our blacks are able workers, but they're ignorant. They can't think for themselves. They wouldn't understand your plans." She paused as if doing a mental roll call. "Mary Jane is the only one I allow inside your office. She's responsible, though not too bright. Once in a while, she shows a whit of common sense, but not very often." She shrugged and spoke as if in an afterthought. "Of course, you do discuss the war with your generals in the reception room. And sometimes during meals."

"Which one is Mary Jane?"

"She's one of the servants who helps in the kitchen. She serves your guests. But she's no one special that you would have remembered. She's also the one who cares for the children."

"Where did she come from?"

"Elizabeth Van Lew suggested her. She said Mary Jane was a good worker and would bring a good rental price. She *is* a good worker."

"You got her from that crazy woman who visits the prisoners at Ligon's and Libby?"

Mary Jane cupped her ear and edged closer to catch the next words. Silence. Her heart skipped a beat, and her feet glued themselves to the floor.

Mrs. Davis raised her voice. "Yes. Elizabeth sent her to me just before she turned daft and began helping our enemies."

President Davis clenched his jaws, and his face reddened. His eyes turned cold and hard. "How long has this Mary Jane been working for you?"

Mary Jane gasped. *President Davis suspects me.*

Before Mrs. Davis could answer, the President banged his fists on the desk again. "I am going to find out who's reporting our plans," he roared, "and when I do...."

Mary Jane spun around and scurried back to the servants' quarters without waiting to hear more. She didn't need to. She understood what would happen.

Once safe inside, she slammed the door, set the bar and tried to breathe.

Massa Davis's threat was more terrifying than her entire first day working for Mistress Davis. She shuddered fearing what would happen if he learned the truth. She must run to Miss Bet for protection, and she had no time to spare. She tore around her room, snatched up her meager possessions, and slipped out into the silent night.

Being out after curfew doubled her fears as she circumnavigated her way through the clogged streets to get to Church Hill. In her haste, she'd neglected to grab a handkerchief. Grimacing, she clapped her hands over her mouth and nose and headed off in the direction she needed to go.

Lantern light leaking through the hospital tents and the reeking air steered her away from the blocked streets where the makeshift infirmaries were. Often she ducked into the shadows to make certain she was not followed.

Her route was lighted only by the third quarter moon until she got beyond the tent area and closer to Church

Hill. What a relief it was to see the first of the gas street lights standing like sentinels of the night, illuminating the Grace Street cobblestones and the red brick sidewalks. Feeling grateful to be almost to her destination, she paused momentarily to catch her breath before hastening on to Miss Bet's mansion. She breathed easier in the less contaminated air as she crept along the wall and around to the back door.

Tap-Tap. Tap-Tap-Tap. Tap-Tap.

Silence. *Maybe Miss Bet was fast asleep by now.*

Tap-Tap. Tap-Tap-Tap. Tap-Tap.

Mary Jane held her breath. Then suddenly the door flew open. She darted inside and sank into the nearest chair until her breathing slowed. Miss Bet prepared her unexpected guest a cup of rye coffee.

"The President's slaves are deserting. Tonight he told Mistress Davis one of us is passing secrets to the North. He suspects me." She took another swallow of the hot, bitter drink. "I must go to Wilson. He'll protect me."

"No, Mary Jane. I can't take you to him. It wouldn't be safe for you...or for him. When President Davis discovers you've run away, the first places he'll look for you are here and at my farm." She laid a comforting hand on her arm. "I'll hide you tonight and get you out of Richmond tomorrow."

Mary Jane gasped. "But what about Wilson? What

about my husband?"

Miss Bet waved off her concern. "Right now my concern is for you, child. You'll be safe sleeping in one of the guest rooms. Before daybreak, you can slip upstairs to the secret chamber. After I bring you breakfast, I'll go down to the Twelfth Street market and see how much of a disturbance your disappearance from the White House has made."

She looked at Mary Jane and spoke with assurance—and a tiny hint of mirth in her voice. "Before this day ends, you will be passed through the lines to City Point, as secretly and carefully as all those detailed war plans you sent to me that Wilson carried to Harrison's Landing."

Fearing that she would never get out of Richmond alive, Mary Jane could not relax. She longed for her precious Wilson. If only she could see him again. She swallowed her tears and prayed. "Please, Lord, let it be so…and please don't let Marse Davis find me."

Mid-morning of the following day, a jumble of enraged voices filtered up from below. Mary Jane couldn't hear what they were yelling until one shrill shriek split the air. "You just wait and see, Miss Van Lew. We'll find her…and she'll wish we had not."

Mary Jane's heart raced so fast, she felt it might explode inside her chest. By coming here, she had endangered her best friend, her mentor.

The little room vibrated as a door slammed angrily. An unsettling quiet enveloped the mansion.

A few minutes later, Miss Bet knocked on the door to the secret attic room. "It's safe to come out now," she said. "They're gone." When Mary Jane opened the door, Miss Bet drew her close to her heart. "You are the smartest and the bravest black woman in Richmond, Mary Jane. You'll never know how much you have helped me with my efforts to free your people." She blinked and then went on. "This war is not yet over, but we will win it because our cause is just."

Miss Bet clenched the muscles along her determined jawline and laid a comforting hand on Mary Jane's shoulder. "This afternoon I will take you to the farm." She paused and then whispered, "Then we'll find Wilson.... So you can say goodbye." She turned to Mary Jane. "You have my promise to send him to you in Philadelphia as soon as I can work that out. Right now it would not be safe for the two of you to travel together."

A flood of tears cascaded down Mary Jane's cheeks, and Miss Bet held her close giving her time to compose herself, before explaining the rest of her plans. "This evening my couriers will pass you safely through our lines to General Grant's headquarters at City Point. My contacts at City Point will see you safely to Philadelphia where my brother will be waiting for you. He will take you to Miss Anna's house, and she and her husband will keep you safe."

Mary Jane studied her face as she explained the plans she had worked out. She trusted her friend with her life.

Miss Bet blinked and swallowed. Then she spoke softly. "I know you've missed Wilson." She continued with a trembling voice. "Until you are together again, remember he has been doing an important job just as you have done."

Mary Jane's lips quivered. Her hands shook. She had to flee Richmond as soon as possible, and she would cling to Miss Bet's promise that she would see Wilson again in Philadelphia. She mopped her tears with the palms of her hands, threw her arms around Miss Bet, and they wept together.

By now nearly every horse in Richmond had been conscripted by the army, including three of Miss Bet's snow-white beauties. Her former social status among the prominent people of the city had enabled her to keep the fourth one. But only by stealth. She had hidden him several times in the smokehouse and several times, inside her mansion. Like all men and beasts in Richmond, he had not had enough to eat the past few years. Now, the scrawny horse did not look like an animal worth stealing.

Nearly everybody in Richmond thought that Miss Bet had lost her senses. Her weird behavior scarcely drew a comment anymore. So no one paid any attention when she left Church Hill in the early afternoon. Her rickety wagon was piled helter-skelter with old rags, broken crockery, a rake minus five teeth, and other nondescript trash.

She was not questioned as she drove her boney nag off in the direction of her farm outside the city. Beneath the trash and the floorboards, Mary Jane Bowser lay hidden from the curious eyes of all. In her left hand, she clutched a little corncob doll. Stuffed into her right pocket was the hair switch given her by Mistress Davis. Having done what she alone could do, she would soon vanish from Richmond as quietly and completely as starlight at sunrise.

While the Emancipation Proclamation paved the way for freedom for all slaves, it did not become a reality until six months after the war ended. On December 6th, 1865, the 13th Amendment to the Constitution was passed, abolishing slavery throughout the United States.

Epilogue

Mary Jane Bowser was a real person, born with an eidetic memory—that's a photographic memory as well as the ability to remember what one hears and repeat it verbatim. Wilson Bowser and Miss Bet (noted Civil War spy Elizabeth Van Lew) were real people, too, and the spy ring Van Lew created in this story was a living underground network, operating primarily in Richmond.

However, until about five years ago, this book could not have been written. Until then details about Mary Jane

Bowser's life were not backed up by adequate documentation. This research was complicated because Mary Jane Bowser used multiple aliases.

Thanks to meticulous research by Drs. Elizabeth R. Varon and Lois Leveen and *New York Times* best-selling author Karen Abbott, fascinating details have emerged. Though some gaps still exist, these three writers unearthed some telling information about Bowser's life after she fled Richmond.

When I began researching the Van Lew-Bowser story about fifteen years ago, my efforts to get documentation directly from Richmond were unsuccessful. One historian quoted Mrs. Jefferson Davis as saying "I had no 'educated negro' in my household." That's how effectively Mary Jane Bowser had fulfilled her role.

Dr. Leveen found in the diary of the Rev. Charles Beecher what is thought to be the only surviving physical description of Mary Jane Bowser. Beecher wrote that she was "a Juno, done in somber marble...her features regular and expressive, her eyes exceedingly bright and sharp, her form and movements the perfection of grace."

Through her research, Dr. Leveen also verified that Generals Ulysses S. Grant, Benjamin Butler, and George H. Sharpe acknowledged the importance of information received from Elizabeth Van Lew. These were details that Mary Jane gathered by keeping alert as she carried out her servant's duties in the Confederate White House.

Referring to Mary Jane Bowser, Elizabeth Van Lew wrote in her diary on May 14, 1864: "When I open my eyes in the morning, I say to the servant, 'What news, Mary?' and my caterer never fails. Most generally our reliable news is gathered from Negroes, and they certainly show wisdom, discretion, and prudence, which is wonderful."

On September 11, 1865, Mary Jane gave a public talk at Abyssinian Baptist Church in Manhattan using the pseudonym Richmonia Richards. An article in the *Brooklyn Eagle* two weeks later, on September 25, 1865, states she gave a public talk at the AME Church on Bridge Street in Brooklyn, New York, under the name Richmonia R. St. Pierre.

According to Dr. Leveen in early 1867, Mary Jane established a freedmen's school in Saint Mary's, Georgia, while referring to herself as Mary Richards.

In a letter to Gilbert L. Eberhart, dated June 1, 1867, Mary Jane said she had married. Henceforth she was to be addressed as Mary J. R. Garvin.

Since Wilson Bowser was one of Miss Bet's couriers, there's a likely possibility that he was captured while delivering one of the Mary Jane's messages he'd received at the farm.

On June 27, Mary Jane wrote Eberhart that she was leaving Saint Mary's, Georgia, possibly to travel to Havana, Cuba. Dr. Leveen was unable to document further information about her. Hence, how and when she died remains a mystery.

On October 6, 1977, citizens gathered to pay tribute to Elizabeth Van Lew, the forgotten spy, at West Farms Soldiers Cemetery in Bronx, New York. The Civil War Memorial Committee unveiled a memorial plaque in her honor. The celebration ended with a Twenty-gun salute by the National Guard.

To protect their secret agents from contempt or hostility after the war, the United States government destroyed their records. Thus, we'll never know precisely everything that Mary Jane Bowser accomplished while spying in the Confederate White House. Still, enough convincing evidence remained that she was worthy of public recognition. On June 30, 1995, she was inducted posthumously into the Military Intelligence Hall of Fame in Fort Huachuca, Arizona. Her citation praised her as "one of the most productive espionage agents of the Civil War."

To enhance dramatic effect, as a novelist, I have taken liberties with the documented information about Miss Bet (Elizabeth Van Lew) and Mary Jane Bowser to create two imagined scenes. I have also tweaked the time frame a bit.

CPSIA information can be obtained
at www.ICGtesting.com
Printed in the USA
LVHW082308120419
614069LV00008B/68/P